Finisterre

Being the Second Part of Two

MICHAEL GILLS

GUIDE DOG
BOOKS

Finisterre © 2021 by Michael Gills

ISBN 978-1-947879-32-4

Library of Congress Control Number:

2013949322

Cover Design by Jennifer Barnes

Guide Dog Books

Bowie, MD

ALSO BY MICHAEL GILLS

Burning Down My Father's House: Stories

West: A Novel

Emergency Instructions: A Novel

The House Across from The Deaf School: Stories

White Indians: Part One

The Death of Bonnie And Clyde and Other Stories

Go Love: A Novel

Why I Lie: Stories

Contents

for Jill and Lyra, always

and for Ron Nehring–*peregrino fuerte*

SYNOPSIS

This is the second part of *White Indians*.

Part One included "What the Newly Dead Don't Know but Learn," and "Earth's First Night," essays which introduce the narrator and crucial elements of a life that has always moved toward Sundance. *White Indians*, a "visionary memoir," recounts Gills' experience as a participant at a Native American Sundance ceremony on Zuni Territory, New Mexico during July 2005. The ceremony unfolds on a wolf refuge and at night. Tending fire, the howling is startling music that informs the text throughout. Sixty men and women dance and pierce themselves during four days, offering flesh to a ninety-feet tall cottonwood, wrapped and glimmering with thousands upon thousands of prayer ties. The breathtaking pageantry of the dance is offset by the shock of seeing flesh offerings taken in the splendor of elaborate costumes and the continuous drumbeat and singing under an enormous sky.

As firekeeper, the narrator is responsible for heating stones for the sacred *inipi*. Later in the dance, a scarred old *heyoka* (backward/forward man) ushers him into the arena where for some time he fans cedar smoke among the dancers under the tree. His perspective is an insider's, riveted by every detail. The result is the first of a two-book work, that places this ceremony in the larger context of Native American prophecy—the return of *Pahana*, lost white brother, and the end of the fourth world.

This second part, Finisterre, recounts a pilgrimage on the Camino de Santiago in north Spain, from Puente la Reina to the ancient cathedral in Santiago de Compostela, said to house the relics of the apostle James—*Iago*—who walked with Christ. And from there the narrative turns toward the bluffs of Finisterre, holy site of initiation, the emotional, spiritual, and physical boundary of the fourth world. *Where earth ends*, the place is called, and so it does. Two tail-pieces conclude the narrative: mother, father and daughter, following the fire priest home; and finally, mid-pandemic in the New World, a surprise afternoon after months of quarantine.

BOOK TWO

Part III

FINISTERRE

1.

The night our house burned, Aunt Gladys woke a hundred miles away with the fire dream full on her, called our number so daddy got up in his underwear just as the roof collapsed, a star-shaped coal already burnt into the heart-side of his chest. She knew—Aunt Gladys *knew.* Uncle Leo could guess cards, I swear. You could see him look at the backside of your hand and know you had the Jack with one eye and a pair of twos. Some people are like that. And my own mother, a decade gone now, she had the dream of flight so many of my people are cursed with, wore herself ragged dodging power lines all the nights of her life. My dreams don't always come to be the way I dream them. Sometimes they're silly-willy or real dark like the one where I wind my way through cracks and crevices where lurks some ancient being that is very much aware of me in every way. And sometimes I taunt this thing, whatever it is, throw a ball of wadded paper into its hole so I hear it rattling and one red eye regards me—and then it comes on with the suddenness of an eclipse penumbra, *O cone of dark descending.* Those nights when I'm visited sometimes coincide with a bellyful of whiskey and a sleepless night or two in advance. These are my sleepwalk nights and, just like Mama, I'm up wandering the house, trying to unlock the mystery of walls that turn into corners and these corners into rooms without doors where the thing itself lies in wait. And just a few nights, this last one in particular, I get led across a river that I never remember crossing by the light of day. Only it's like dying, I know that. And this last time, when I awoke

11

on the hard rock bank of the other side, shivering on an ancient alluvial fan before first light in mid-October, I woke myself yelling *help, help, help*.

From the other side, my rescuers heard my call, spotlighted me, and drifted a raft to where I lay beside a boulder on Ledge Rapid, the San Juan River down at Four Corners, three shattered ribs, but dry. I'd somehow crossed deep water, the bend in the channel, without getting wet.

This is the story of how we were pilgrims on the Camino de Santiago, me, Jill, and our fifteen-year-old daughter, Lyra. How we biked across the north of Spain from Puente la Reina to the cathedral at Compostela, and then, with the ashes of a dead boy, to earth's end at Finisterre.

We'd reached a crossroads.

Jill and I'd both hit fifty, dizzied by how time does backflips on you, how it gets up and goes, and even though you've been hearing how time flies your whole life, it's different when you actually see it happening. Together, we'd gone west, across the Mississippi and blue sky Wyoming with its Rodeo Weekend and combination drug, liquor and gun stores, to Utah, where I worked through a Ph.D. and spent three days a week teaching in classrooms where through the window glass shone the Wasatch Mountains, lightning topped, golden sometimes and at others pink alpenglow, a word I learned for morning light on a snow peak. Lyra came screaming on a full moon night in January, and we'd done good by her, put her through Montessori at four fifty a pop per month, and then the Open Classroom School where I co-op taught her classes from first through fifth grades and learned, for maybe the first time, that I was not a bad man, that I was capable of good. When Mama died, well that was a whole other deal that there was no preparing for and I went crazy for a while, lost and wandering, and the Indian business, what they call the Red Road, helped pull me out of the fall. Something about the intergalactic void of the *inipi* lodge, the fierce heat of the *tunkas*, and the rolling thunder song eased my being.

I found myself charged with various addicts, alcoholics, oddballs and sundry outcasts just like myself, freaks one and all come to worship at the foot of the neon cross or, in this case, a sweat lodge in Rose Park, Utah. There was a big-breasted man, I'm swearing to God, thirty-eight D maybe, who'd crawl in behind Gloria, the one real Indian in our group. She's Lakota, from Green Grass where Chief Arvel Lookinghorse keeps the White Buffalo Calf *canupa*, she smells like fry bread and the sprig of sage tucked behind an ear. They take the east hotspot so the firelight shines on their faces, then comes Ricky with the claw necklace—chicken? eagle? corded around his neck, fresh from rehab, then Joe and Carl and the tattooed girl with the see-through skirt. To my right, my good wife Jill, the tiny bells on the cedar bag jingling, and Lyra, our teenager, whose moon has come flooding over us.

In the doorway, fireman's face. "You ready for water? *Mini wakan?*"

"Yeah," I say. "*Mini wakan.*"

And there we go—on solstice and equinox and whenever anyone's sick or somebody they love is about to die or is dead, or before certain job interviews or Lyra's ear surgery. The call is made. I gather drum and *canupa*, fresh sage from the backyard and suffer myself to earth and air, fire and water.

And it all somehow worked.

Then, one morning an old man stared at me though my own eyes. I'd sleepwalked my way into a corner where a Martin D-28 leaned, tuned to a straight E, mewed a little with every nudge. This was November 2012 in Salt Lake, the snow'd started to fly, the tomatoes were still blooming in the backyard—odd, the bright yellow blooms under a late fall sun as the arctic, melted beyond human memory, began to refreeze.

Peg, Jill's mother, had died that May, and her passing was not an easy one. That numb lostness I'd felt when Mama went, the disbelief then anger then grief, breathed its way into our house again, and by New Year's collapsed on my front porch in the form of a high-heeled party girl in a cocktail dress, blonde hair spilling over bare shoulders on my woodpile. She lay there crying *God, oh God, please help me* and it was after midnight New Year's Eve and we were asleep, dead to the world, 2013, the new year arrived. The January cold had sailed over us that week, ten below zero outside, death-of-exposure-weather for passed out drunks and homeless, derelict addicts who hadn't made it to the Odyssey house, and for this party girl in her pale blue dress who cried out maybe thirty minutes shy of her own river crossing. She was nineteen, maybe twenty, not far from Lyra.

Too much Led Zep in the 70's, my hearing's fried.

Jill and Lyra have both been prescribed hearing aids. Ours is a house hard of hearing. So it was by fluke her voice came to me, and I heard her out there rattling hunks of wood and praying, *please open the door, please open the door*, and in her voice the realization that no one would.

Inside, she miraculously produced a phone, auto-dialed help. On the way out, she handed three dollars from the old parka I'd zipped her into. She was crying.

"I'll bring this coat back tomorrow," she said, and I never saw her again, though the parka lay on the woodpile next day, the inebriate smell of her on it. A whiff of vomit.

A week later, my beard turned gray. Overnight. I woke up and there I was in the mirror. Something had to give.

Charlie and Dwight Butler run a bike shop I pass on the way to the liquor store of which there are precious few in Utah, liquor stores that is. Sometimes I stop on the way home if it's not quite happy hour or someone's birthday is coming up, which it was—Lyra's 15th—and it was there I first saw the advertisement of a mountain bike juxtaposed against a cathedral: *Bike Across Spain*, it said, and my first thought: *why the fuck not?*

I'd learn that the *Camino* had been traversed forever. It was said to lead to the oldest pagan initiation site on the planet, that half a million pilgrims walked the way annually a thousand years ago. From France to the Atlantic, it cut the whole of Spain. After the trek from Navarro to Rioja, Leon and Galacia, the pilgrimage wound to the foot of the thousand-year-old cathedral on the poster whose gothic towers were claimed to stand over the headless corpse of *Iago*, St. James, the fisherman who'd walked with Christ and proselytized along the *Camino* himself. Beheaded by Herod

Agrippa, story was that friends put his body on a boat without sails that somehow floated across the Mediterranean, through Gibraltar, and down the Iberian coast to Galacia and the mouth of the river Ulla near Iria Flavia which, because of silting, was now an estuary but once was the coast. There, under a field of stars—*Compostela*—the body lay for 750 years.

A hermit shepherd followed music and lights to a place where he dug and found bones that were later authenticated as the Apostle James. Around the hillside tomb grew the city of Santiago which drew pilgrims straight away. During the battle with Moors at Clavijo, the pivotal moment when defeat was at hand, *Iago* appeared atop a white stallion wielding a sword like fire and was ever after known as *Matamoros*—killer of Moors, patron saint of Spain.

It was a good story, and miracles were said to happen along the way. Guidebooks listed a whole slew of dead people who rose up, blind who suddenly beheld enemies and were borne up on the wings of storks that nested in church belfries. The Holy Grail was said to be housed in a church on top of the mountain pass of O'Cebreiro. Wine fountains sprung from stones along the way. Still, hospitals were far apart and ancient cemeteries with unmarked pilgrim graves speckled the maps. Prisoners, *murderers even*, were forgiven jail time to walk the *Camino*. The Gills were not bike people—the tight jerseys and crotch-grabbing shorts seemed silly. How could such craziness come upon us? What could we possibly hope to find on the *Camino* where walked pilgrims for every reason imaginable? Of the three of us, only Lyra was Spanish fluent. We were not wealthy. Who on earth could afford two-thousand dollar plane tickets?

Jill said *yes* without batting an eye. We'd gathered at the table on the 15th of January, 2013, the deadline for deciding. "Listen to your heart," she said. "What does your heart say?"

All night in the air, the three of us stumbled with our heavy-wheeled suitcases from the guts of the *aeropuerto* to blue sky Madrid, we were immediately recognized as *peregrinos* by our scallop shells and hailed *buen camino*! A bus drove us to town square where we walked into some sort of protest march, a whole stream of folk dressed in cardboard bull heads, screaming *trabajo* and *liberdat* and *silencio no mas*. There were policemen on either side of us and the brick street that was old beyond belief, stones set, I'd learn, by Imperial Rome in the day of Augustus Caesar. We passed a statue of the poet Lorca in a square where people sat in the open eating trayfuls of tapas and drinking wine with these big cloth sheets flapping from stone verandas that looked like cathedrals. Bells were ringing and troops of gypsy singers and dancers sashayed past—our first shining hour in Madrid. Lyra spun on a heel and pointed at a door claiming to be the residence of Cervantes, the exact premises where Don Quixote and Sancho Panza came into this world in the city where a king and queen inhabited a palace on a hill amidst a hundred-acre hunting wood where thrived the most beautiful birds on earth for shooting.

We wandered, dazed.

By some stroke of magic Jill guided us straight to the door of hotel *Mucure Santo Domingo*. Lyra's Spanish was good enough to get us to our room, the walls of which were painted in black light neon, an aquarium as seen from the inside out surrounded by colorful swimming fish and blue water, coral, a giant squid spewing purple ink, the ceiling a sky seen through water. Above my head, the depth of ocean crashed into dreamless fish-sleep, gills trembling as wind on wings.

Our guidebook was written by a priest (or was he a mystic?) who encouraged *peregrinos* to bring and discard the dead weight of their lives. To reconcile inner and outer realities, this mystic-priest said that we must learn to turn loose. I'd brought one of Mama's business cards. It was pale blue, I remember, with her name embossed just to the right of a map of the U.S. and Arkansas emboldened: Support Services Manager, Arkansas Department of Finance & Administration, and on the back, Mike, Love you! Mama. Another identical card says See You for Thanksgiving Dinner, Love, and another is blank, the phone number now answered by her replacement who is not amused on days when I dial her up and do not speak. The cards are in my pocket when we tour the palace and then the Prado before being driven north and east from Madrid to Puente la Reina where we'll claim bicycles, don tight garb and head west. Jill and Lyra—they've brought things to turn loose of too, I know, and the rest of our party, still strangers. But I had Mama's blue cards, writing from her hand.

There is a painting in *Museo Nacional del Prado* in Madrid—a rather large painting situated at eye level by Diego Rodriquez Silva Velazquez—titled *Las Meninas*, a representation of the artist standing before a life-sized easel gazing straight into your face, brush in hand, as if you posed for him. King Philip the IV's young daughter stares as well, bathed in light, along with her maids, a dwarf and dog, attendants—stunningly rendered—and the faded faces of the king and queen which hover ghostlike in a mirror on the room's far side. The long-dead painter's gaze freezes the viewer so that one is simultaneously subject and audience, an effect so potent that Picasso reproduced the piece fifty-eight times in one year, 1956, the three hundredth year since its painting.

There is no need to dwell on the work—you will no doubt study it one day.

Except to say that we'd viewed it three separate times on the day the charter bus drove us to Puente la Reina, Basque country at the foot of the Pyrenees where we were to join a group of cyclists as pilgrims on the Camino de Santiago. All day on the bus, the road north through wide-open country strewn with blood-red poppies, thousand-year-old churches would rise up out of nowhere, a real shock. And I kept picturing Velazquez with the cross of St. James painted on his chest by King Philip after his death, a gesture that lifted him to a sacred order, only he never knew—or did he?—the look on his face, the attendant come to call at the far door—how will you be remembered?

The artist offers eternity.

That afternoon we saw our first pilgrims.

Outside *Alburgue Jakue*, on the east side under a shade tree away from the sun, they were red-faced and exhausted at the end of the day, collapsed, some of them, in the grass. I traced the path they'd walked through a wide pasture cut by a creek, over tree-lined fields east and west to where the arched bridge built by a queen whose name had been forgotten marked the Camino itself, a dirt track beat into the earth through the millennium by saints and martyrs, murderers, King Ferdinand and Isabella *Catalico* who was said to have knee-walked the last thirty feet on a stone floor in Santiago de Compostela, and there she placed her hand on a time-stained statue of Iago, an act repeated so many times that a groove was worn into the Italian marble to the depth of a hand. They lay half dead with heat stroke it seemed. There was something right and sustaining in their exhaustion, or so it seemed, a light in their faces.

"God," Jill'd said when I called her over.

Lyra just shook her head, she didn't speak.

We had our photograph taken beside a bronze statue of Santiago, pilgrim staff in hand, rocks piled in front of him for the burdens we'd bear. And there we are, three, smiling at the camera where it all began, knowing nothing of what will come.

We dine in the great hall that night on fish and ham seven ways, the olives and cheese and fresh loaves of peasant bread slathered in butter, bottles of red and white wine floating from one end of our company's table to the other. We meet NiNi and Ron, a Utah Supreme Court Justice who once played football at Cornell and ran the 800 for the Chicago Track Club. There was Ray Thomason, from Texas, a liver transplant surgeon who asked me if the University of Arkansas was a two-year college. With him, Liz, a wiry Utah blonde who'd been an aid for Reagan in D.C. A pretty realtor with fierce legs was named Merrilee, accompanied by a chiropractor who'd brought a portable table and various muscle stimulators and inhibitors and probably a whole lot of pills in case we got hurt, which we did, a lot. Janine, a museum curator, had quit her job, the *Camino* her burning of bridges. There's Christoph, a co-leader of the quest, and his wife Taunya Lasagna— how she introduced herself. Fernando Rubio was from Oviedo, a Spanish professor at the University of Utah who'd biked the Camino three times and would now lead our party toward Logroño and Burgos, Leon in three days. We'd dub him El Cid and his one-forked bike Biebeca—his wife Lucia was to meet us mid-pilgrimage. Our bus driver, Ramon, spoke not a word of English, and, like everyone else we met, was sweet as pie and would carry our gear in the belly of the charter bus and save our asses should we falter, which we did. And there was us—Jill, Lyra, and me—listening to our hearts. Isn't that what we were doing?

The first hill was a killer.

Over the six fine arches of Queen's bridge, we pedaled past the convent with its white wimpled nuns to where the hill Fernando'd warned of rose up from scrub wood. The Camino was narrow, rutted, the trees low on either side. The Judge and NiNi had left early to walk the hardship before light and meet us at the bridge over the poison river, where men had historically waited with knives to skin the horses that drank from the water and died. The bikes were new to us—Specialized Rockhoppers which we'd never ridden before, so the seats and handlebars were all out of adjustment, and already my ass, *mi culo*, hurt like hell. Bill, the preacher man, was off his already, pushing uphill, enormous belly heaving. Merrilee and Kevin, they'd escorted the judge. Jill crashed first, a hard thwack in the rutted gravel, and then the three of us were off walking, legs on fire, pushing the rise, sucking water, Lyra with that look like we were all crazy people. After a mile, more, the hill still came at us. Here was a hill where pilgrims had died, I was sure of it, the veins in my wife's neck blue through her skin. And it was at that moment, when the pain of this first stage was about to eat our lunch, that we turned a corner and there walked Jesus, white robe blood-spattered from the crown of thorns, dragging a wooden cross. It was a *real* cross, a goddamn load, and this guy had his shoulders down, the tendons stretched tight in his calves and I could see where the crossbar had rubbed him raw on both shoulders. I wanted to help him, give him water, take on part of his load. But what do you say to a man who has chosen to drag a cross up a mountainside? What words are there for *Jesus*?

Finally, we hit the top. Bill climbed on his bike, thunka-thunked away.

Lyra said, "This is bullshit, Dad. People don't do this."

Jesus was coming.

I could hear him grunting, the butt of the cross whacking the gaps between stones, and behind him came a whole throng of folk bearing staffs and white scallop shells clicking from their shoulders, every color and type of people you could imagine, one with a medicine wheel emblazoned on his chest, the black, red, yellow and white of the Lakota Nation, the Red Road here on Camino. Some rode horses, donkeys even. We'd ride past John the Baptist, the three Marys, Shadrach, Meshach and Abednego.

Jill labored just before them.

"You can do it. You've got this," I said, but I didn't believe it, two hours into the thing, five-hundred kilometers in front of us, the dust already heavy on my tongue.

Then Jill reached us, red-faced.

"Come on," she said.

Janine pushed up beside her, we were not alone. The way flattened and we passed a flag where waved the bars of Aragon and the chains of Navarro, the yoke and arrows for King Ferdinand and Isabella, toward Rio Salado, the planned meeting at the poison river.

2.

Where the bridge arched highest sat a woman whose flowing red hair was tied in blue ribbons, selling tuna sandwiches on wheat bread and iced lemonade, a whole slew of pilgrims taking lunch with bare feet soaking between rocks in the flowing river. It was hot, the sun straight overhead and fierce. The judge had made it, NiNi and Merrilee, they'd ridden on with the plan being for us to all meet up in Estella at the famed wine fountain. The water was clean and blue over my feet, nothing about it seemed poisonous in the least. It was a creek, really, the sort Mama's brother Uncle Larry used to haul us to afternoons in Arkansas, when we'd swing off a rope tied to a tree on a high bank, and he'd make us fistfight whatever hillbilly kids were there with their whiskey swilling daddies. Preacher Bill'd ridden off already and Christoph was herding the rest of us together on the hillside over the bridge. He was waving at me, as were Jill and Lyra—Michael, come on, get up here. Dad, it's time. But I sat there for a while with the blue cold water running over my feet, and I was tempted to drink, the red-headed woman calling out to hungry pilgrims from the high-arched bridge.

The guidebook written by the mystic-priest offers the warning: *If the weather is hot, the stretch through Estella to Los Arcos can be exhausting.* Goddamn straight. We pedaled a Roman road uphill through a thick brier, then thunka-thunked downhill, the cantilevered stones jarring my teeth together until Liz—the Utah blonde—crashed ahead of us, red blood running down her arm until Christoph wrapped it with gauze and tape and we rode on.

Bill, the retired preacher who'd say last rights for any of us should we fall, had disappeared who knows where. We wound down alongside the Ega River, me and Jill, mid-afternoon maybe, the chafing that would turn raw between my crotch and thigh burning already. The city of Estella appeared far below to the north, old-looking with remnants of four castles on four hills in the cardinal directions. The water in our bottles was hot. We were thirsty, red-faced, sunburned already and I think we'd forgot to eat—I don't think we'd eaten since breakfast back in Puente la Reina. Our company was scattered, only the three of us and Janine—who rode slower than we were, even—were left together. On either side of the Camino grew bushes and sometimes cherry trees bright with red fruits, and there were fences and horses grazing in pastures that undulated off into hills and the world seemed big then to me. The mystic-priest had exalted at the famed wine fountain at the Bodega de Irache where pilgrims were invited to *beber sin abusar te invitamos con agrado*. We were to meet there, at the wine fountain, and decide whether or not to ride the last stage of the day to Logroño, or to bag it, kick back in the air-conditioned bus and let Ramon drive us to the hotel and seven course meal Fernando had set up.

We arrived to sip the cool wine of Bodega de Irache alone.

Lyra had fallen back with Janine. It was nearly four, blazing under the sun, when we threw our bikes down, emptied water bottles and filled them with the clean, cold wine. Jill and I leaned against a shaded wall, facing the Camino as it fell away before us. "Here's to happiness," I said, drank half a water bottle and refilled.

She said, "Like hell," and drank.

The wine was good. What I didn't know was that all along the way, when we least expected, there'd be carts of iced lemonade and pasta salads, breads and cheese and, yes, sometimes wine, even, for weary pilgrims, a thousand-year -ld tradition subsidized by the Spanish government.

"They're watching us," Jill said. She'd emptied and refilled her bottle as well. A video camera's one gleaming eye shined down from above the fountain. She held her bottle up and toasted. "Vitality," she said.

Bill, the big-bellied jolly priest, I'd known him two days and that was long enough to know that he loved wine above all things, and that he was genuinely looking forward to being where we were that second.

Jill said, "This is hard. I could sleep this second."

"My ass hurts," I said, and the wine was cold and good and I could drink a gallon of it, I was sure. "My balls."

Though we didn't know it, Ramon and the bus were parked just around the corner beside a grass park where we'd pray soon for lost Bill, that he might be kept safe, shepherded, that he might have sustenance and spiritual fortitude, that he might toast to happiness with the good red wine of Irache, that our private parts might be soothed, that this day might yet end well, and that more wine would soon come our way.

"What did you bring?"

"Bring?"

Beside the wine spigot was one labeled water, which a peregrino with the staff and derelict hat I'd come to recognize as emblems of Santiago fills up with, giving us, on our third water bottles, the eye.

"To get rid of?"

Lyra appeared in the distance, my good, sweet-hearted daughter and her newfound friend Janine. The world was good and this was the best place to be, beside the fountain of life in Spain, on our way to Logroño, Burgos the next night with its mighty cathedral where lay the bones of El Cid the most brave.

"Ray," I said, "The surgeon. He's got a bagful of ashes. He's spreading someone along the Camino."

"Like the movie."

The man wanted us to take his picture by the fountain. Lyra and Janine pedaled up, threw their bikes down beside ours and fell into the shade. Janine sighed, said nothing.

"Where is everyone?" Lyra wanted to know.

A Missing Persons Report was filed at the Police Station in Estella, while we waited in a circle on the green grass, a good hundred yards away from the red wine fountain, thank be. Bill, it turned out, had been sighted, stopped and spoken to even, on the main highway some fifteen kilometers away, and then he'd disappeared. The question we had to debate, there in the circle on the grass, was what in hell to do next. Should we ride the final stage of the day to Logroño and Las Arcos, and the hotel with its soft beds that awaited us? Should we scrap riding altogether, set out in the bus on the main highway west in search of the lost priest? Should we drink more pilgrim wine and think about it? Lyra made up her mind fast, stowed the Rockhopper in the bus hull, collapsed in a reclining seat beside the Judge and NiNi. Janine followed Lyra up into the bus. So it was Jill and me, Fernando Rubio, Christoph and Taunya Lasagna, Kevin and Merrilee—who it turned out were master-level bikers who race from Salt Lake across the Salt Flats to Nevada yearly in the Tour de Utah—Texas Ray and Liz. Except for Kevin and Merrilee, and Fernando—I don't remember if he'd had his fill or not—we'd all drunk right much wine.

We decided to bike the last stage to Logroño. We didn't understand, neither Jill nor I, the hill that lay before us. Who's looking at maps when there's such wine to be had?

From the back window of the receding bus, Lyra waved, and there was Janine beside her, waving, big huge smiles on their faces. We were to meet at the ice cream shop beneath Hotel Bracos in Logroño, capital of Rioja.

Beyond Estella, the climb began. On a wide open treeless plain the rolling hills were covered in green grass and a sea of still, red poppies. The rest of our party—Kevin and Merrilee, Fernando, Taunya, Liz and Ray, real bikers all—had bolted, knowing that the trick to a hill is to charge. Only Christoph held back with Jill and me, in the easy gears, slow-mo pedaling up the dusty Camino that shined and disappeared ahead of us in the afternoon heat. We had the sense, I'm glad, to wash the wine out and refill our water bottles, which we sucked dry far before the top, when we were both hurting and red faced and thinking about the air-conditioned bus, Janine and Lyra with their seats reclined, Ramon cruising down the road to the ice cream shop. At times like this, gutting it out, we don't talk, me and Jill. She tucked in behind me and I knew she wouldn't quit. We'd been like this forever—the competitive swimmer in her blood, hiking to the four lakes basin in the high Uintas, the trail straight up and the lactic acid on fire in our legs, miles like this, and we're stupid, new to Utah and the Brook Trout in Four Lakes Basin, and we're both humping cast-iron skillets in our backpacks so I can fry them, stupid Arkie that I am. And she won't quit, she's never quit.

24

And then I dragged her out in tight riding pants with the pads built into the butt, to ride five hundred miles and be a pilgrim on the Camino and the only way she'd quit would be to die, and we've both drunk a bucketful of wine, and after a solid hour climbing in the bright sun, in the easy gears but not stopping, Christoph encouraging us though he's barely broken a sweat, that's what I was thinking, that we might die, as so many pilgrims have, right there on that very hill.

Christoph passed Jill a power bar, a full water bottle from one of the saddle bags on either side of his mountain bike. He missed his daughter who they dropped off in Germany with his parents on the way. He grew up in the Black Forest, home of the Big Bad Wolf, Hansel and Gretel, Goldilocks, all that Three Bear stuff—they all came out of the Black Forest, where they sometimes went on beer-drinking binges when he was in college and they'd haul in barrels of black beer and stay drunk for days in the gloom and magic.

Jill's polite—it's in her blood. Even if she was dying, if someone talked to her, she'd talk back. She'd cut my throat with the lid of a tin can, but it is not possible for her to be rude on purpose in public, even in the midst of very real heat stroke, even when her heart rate had maxed out and she would fall out any second.

She told Christoph about her time in Berlin, how when she'd graduated college, her parents had bought her a Eurorail pass, and she'd gone off with a backpack and a General's daughter, and they'd stayed there for a while with German boys who always had good beer.

I wouldn't stop unless she did. And Christoph had her mind off it now, the pain. For anybody who hasn't bucked fifty miles on a mountain bike on Roman roads and mountains, past wine fountains and churches like these big make-believe places from fairy tales your mother read you back in Lonoke County, a million years ago and miles away—Billy Goat's Gruff, the troll with long knives under the bridge—it hurts, and then the body goes numb.

And just when I saw spots, and the heat turned to a chill at the base of my back and I could no longer feel my ass nor balls nor legs even, and the German boys had morphed into Italian boys who touched her in all the wrong places, a shaded room of stone materialized beside the Camino, with a deep pool of water where stairs descended, and the three of us lay our bikes down and collapsed. The shade was immediate relief. Jill went down on her back. Like a sack of grain. And it was as if we'd been plucked from the world of hurt, given reprieve for no reason of our own merit. The hilltop shelter was built into the ground where a stone chamber was filled with spring water from below. We were not alone. How many had come before us to this exact moment?

There, just inside the chamber, Ray leaned.

"What is this place," Jill said.

At the top of the brutal hill, how steep it had been and hot and she'd overheated, her face bright red and heart pounding. I'd seen spots, gone chill and then numb. The spring was constructed for just such a moment—it appeared at the instant when one could go no further, the height of need. The stone-cold shelter gathered us. I stepped down to the water, soaked a red bandana and lay it over Jill's forehead.

"Grace," Ray said.

"God, thank you," Jill said, and we rested that way for a while, and Ray told us the story of his lost son, the one whose ashes he had brought to the Camino. His was a southern voice, soothing. So close to heat stroke, the words echoed off the far wall, somehow out of order and I couldn't understand anything beyond that there had been a priest who'd given the son baseball cards, and that the son had hanged himself.

For some reason I thought of snakes, copperheads, the summer I'd laid a flagstone sidewalk for this lady who had me quarry rock from her back pasture, and how the serpents lay underneath, whole nests sometimes, big as beach balls.

I saw why—the shade was holy, and light played on the water. A healing spring from thin air when I thought that we'd die.

My first day on the Camino as a pilgrim, in the year 2013, the 26th of June, when I was 52 and on the verge of becoming someone I didn't know but had always suspected, ended in an all-out bike race with Fernando Rubio who flew downhill behind me so I could hear his tires crunching gravel. The healing cave had cooled my blood, and my energy all came flooding back. I rode like hell down into Los Arcos where Ramon had parked the bus idling in a lot where we'd load the bikes and be driven to Logroño. We raced to the bus, me and Fernando, and I made crazy turns, the front wheel skittering, chattering, about to throw me for a loop, but I hung on. All those Sundays training, when we'd ride Emigration Canyon, up beside the creek with its waving willows where I'd once found the skeleton of a huge whitetail, a twelve pointer, dead under the willows we were harvesting for a new lodge, and I had wondered if it was bad medicine to cut willows from around the carcass of an animal whose blood and sinew had rotted into the ground, been sucked up by the willow people, would this be the lodge of death? Would the deer spirit manifest in ceremony? The three of us, me, Jill and Lyra, we'd pedal the eight miles up to a gravel lot that overlooked a blue reservoir, and we'd be hurting, terribly. The Mormons had constructed a stone plaque up there commemorating their descent into the Salt Lake valley, how the Donner party had made it to within half-a-mile only to turn around, take the longer route to the Sierra Nevada that sealed their fate.

I felt Fernando behind me. Lyra was on a bench outside the bus, drinking a Slurpee with NiNi and Ron, Janine. A policeman—was there a policeman?

"You're ready to ride another stage. Aren't you?"

Fernando pulled beside me and we rode the rest of it together. Kevin met me with an ice cold beer in one chiropractor hand, one for me in the other. We fell down on a bench. Jill would come soon, Ray and Liz. We'd be shuttled to town, the hotel and first Camino meal together. Lyra's happy not to have ridden the last nineteen miles. She offered me Slurpee and a hug. The rest of us—I saw them descending the long downhill, Jill's silver helmet shining, making good time. There was a pilgrim with the same big guidebook as me—*he's a mystic*, she says, *for sure a mystic*.

"Priest," I say, and still there was no Bill.

The bus ride to Logroño, I don't remember a bit of it, those thirty, forty miles, save that the coach got real quiet and all the seats reclined and everyone just seemed to give out. We were not a young party. Ron and NiNi'd hit their mid-sixties, Ray and Liz weren't far behind, nor Janine, Bill was sixty if a day, Merrilee and Kevin, early fifties like me and Jill. Fernando, Christoph, Taunya Lasagna—they were all bucking forty, maybe forty-five for Fernando. Of us all, Lyra was the only one young in years, and that had made her an early favorite among the pilgrims, to spend her fifteenth summer on the dusty Camino, on a bike that chafed so terribly between the legs, breathing the dirt from pilgrim's feet with such an unforgiving sun above the hard Roman road below. I believe she gave the others hope, especially Ron and NiNi, who'd once ridden from St. Petersburg to Paris, and Ron had played football for Cornell, been a track star, his name on a sign outside Kalamazoo, Michigan that said Welcome to Kalamazoo, Home of Derrick Jeter and Ron Nehring. But that was all a long time ago, the glory days when NiNi sewed patchwork into her jeans, braided her hair and memorized every word of "Diamonds and Rust." Having a young person along, especially Lyra with her good heart and open embrace, enticed them to remember how it had been for them when strength came easy, as it did not today, the first day of the Camino on a bike, riding after a stroke, this was the last hurrah for them, Ron and NiNi.

Jill was flat out behind me, sprawled across a whole seat, shoes off big swollen feet. There was the smell of us collectively, what Ramon must have thought up front, behind the wheel with the four-foot mirror above so he could see us all, what a company we must have appeared to him, rolling into Logroño, fifty miles under our belts that first day, who gave a rat's ass. It was quiet and the bus was cool. Our hotel room was reserved for a party of three—two queens with a window overlooking the square. There was the dinner ahead, which really meant something now, having burned so many calories, food was important, not to be taken lightly—and the Spanish, if anyone, knew how to do food and wine, the many courses entangling. I was delirious, plumb silly.

"Daddy," Lyra called. "Dad."

She sat up front, behind Ramon, who had just come to a halt outside our hotel door, beside which, as promised, was an ice cream shop with a fancy wooden bench in front where leaned a blue Rockhopper with saddle bags. And there sat Bill, the priest, in a tight blue shirt with a cathedral on front—just like ours—licking the top scoop of a double vanilla ice cream cone, this serene look on his face as if we were the ones who'd been lost and our prodigal return was just how it was supposed to happen.

3.

The first miracle of the Camino, Fernando pronounced, over lamb shank and the wine of Rioja poured deep into the glasses. After dinner, low in our chairs, the twelves of us sat, passing the sweet seventh of eight opened bottles of Rioja, when we were feeling good and had washed off the road dirt and sweat and blood, and we'd not thought far enough ahead to know that we'd do it all again tomorrow and the next day and the day after that.

"Speech," Christoph said.

And beside him Ray Thomason said, "Here, here," and clinked his silver fork into the wine glass. "Speech," he too said, and Bill, a big man florid with the day's sun and now lamb and wine, he stood up at the head of the table and said with a sweetness that I had not foreseen, "I was lost. It was a shepherd found me."

Our table was in the lower floor of a restaurant in downtown Logroño, and we'd walked through the noisy tables of hungry Spaniards to get there, many of whom were looking at us now from above, waiting for what came next. Bill had an audience. I believe he was used to such.

The whole place held its breath.

He'd lost us on the Roman Road, a braid in the Camino that happens every so often when shop keepers set up the yellow arrows to guide confused pilgrims on their way, so there are many Caminos that are one.

He'd walked for a while. He'd pushed his bike. I remembered him crashing during our practice ride on the rail trail in Park City, how he'd ridden hard into a curb and flipped over the handlebars, so Christoph had had to unwrap a new med kit and doctor him right there on the road, not a half mile into the ride. Today there had been a field of purple flowered clover and it was quiet and peaceful and he'd had the urge to lay down and sleep for a while, like we had in the shaded room of cool water. I could understand that. I could hear it in his voice. "*God, thank you,*" Jill had said.

"When I woke up he was standing over me. 'Who are you?'" Bill'd asked.

"A shepherd. Would you like tea?"

And this Spanish shepherd had walked him to a cottage and brewed green tea so that Bill was wonderfully restored. He told the man that he'd been a priest, a sort of shepherd himself, and how odd and beautiful that this one had been sent to him now, in his time of need.

The shepherd had pointed the direction to Logroño via the highway, where the police had stopped Bill and talked to him so that Fernando knew he'd been sighted. But the fifty miles of highway to Logroño—who could say? How could Bill ride that on a mountain bike and beat us to the punch? It had happened—he'd been there with the tranquil look in his eye, licking a double scoop of ice cream, *the first miracle of the Camino.*

Thursday, 27 June, we wake in the room with lengths of cord we've tied wall-to-wall still dripping with the clothes Jill's washed in the sink, a big, nice room with a bed for Lyra and the Spanish bathroom with its curtain-less shower and twin toilet bidet. The hotel was modern, lots of squares and art on the walls, blues and reds and mute yellows—Marques de Vallejo, the sign an MV embedded on a scallop shell that got stamped in red on my *Ano de la Fe* where my name and a fish were printed under *Nombre del per-egrino*—proof of my passage. As we would learn to do each day, the three of us slathered Butt Butter on the apple-sized rashes that burned between our legs, sifted Monkey Butt powder onto the wounds and squeezed into the damp cycling pants with the padded ass now molded into the shape of our bicycle saddles. We rubbed on sunscreen, limped to the elevator pulling suitcases hastily crammed shut, and were delivered to the quiet dining hall with its breakfast of boiled eggs and ham, good strong coffee and melon, the hot chocolate Lyra loved called *Cola Cao,* and toast, lots of buttered toast run through a metal conveyer.

"Good morning," I said.

Across from me Jill yawned. Lyra groaned. She'd be in ninth grade next fall. Ninth grade—I remembered ninth grade, blow drying my hair, shaving, trying not to get caught staring at sixteen-year-old girls who'd grown into goddesses over summer—Debbie Boyle, how she'd babysat at a house in Cabot where I poured a concrete house slab beyond the pool deck, how she'd lay back in the chaise lounge in a purple bikini and pretend she didn't see me in cutoffs and a hand trowel, and I'd talked her into letting me wear one of her rings, and you could see it shining on my ring finger in that year's football picture, turquoise—real from New Mexico, she'd said.

"*Buenos dias, Padre,*" Lyra said.

"*Buenos dias, Hija.*"

Cola Cao—proof of the Spanish conquest of the New World, how Moctezuma had drunk it by the gallon mixed with blood and it had given him great strength, it seemed to the conquistadors. Lyra will ride across Spain on a burst of Cola Cao.

Ramon ate fast. He pulled the bus up in front and honked, so the whole lot of us had our *anos* stamped, suitcases stored in the bus bin underneath where the bikes leaned one into another, walked to the seats with our sweat on them and collapsed to sleep. That day we would witness the miracle of the hanged innocent in *Santo Domingo De la Calzada* where chickens inhabited a cathedral with the chains and handcuffs from freed prisoners, presided over by a Canaanite giant—Cristobal—who'd served Satan until discovering the Devil feared Christ, and for the rest of his life carried pilgrims across the river, his image painted ten feet tall near the doorway.

It was dark inside the church in Santo Domingo de la Calzada, and high beside a retablo, embedded in a thick wall, colorful chickens clucked behind a pane of glass—the thirty-third generation relatives of those from the miracle legend. Story was, this family of German pilgrims—father, mother and son—stopped for the night and the innkeeper's daughter came on to the boy who turned her down flat. She hid silver in his pack and had him arrested for theft next morning, and they hanged the boy, left him on the rope to rot as a warning to thieves. The heartbroken parents had nothing to do but make their way on to Compostela where they prayed for sonny's soul at pilgrim's mass. On the way back, they passed the town again and could not keep from the execution platform where their son, good as new, hung gleefully, his weight supported all those days by the hermit saint, Santo Domingo.

The parents ran to the Mayor's apartment, screaming *miracle, miracle* and the perturbed old man, roasting his chicken dinner, said that the boy hanging in the courtyard was about as alive as that chicken roasting in the oven, whereupon the bird cocka-doodle-dooed, flapped from the oven door off the veranda and into the cathedral where it was ever after counted holy. "Dad," Lyra said. "You think it's true?"

Our first stage of day two, it was early, the heat not on yet, and I'd had a beer with Christoph at a stop on the way. The chickens were nice. They were taken care of, and there was the painting of the giant at the doorway behind us, and the admonishment to take bread to the chickens for the love of God, signed by Afonso of Castilla.

Who could know what was possible in such a place?

That day we topped a hill at noontime and the land fell away in a panorama so I spun on a foot gazing on the fields of blood-red poppies that sloped down to a far-off church shining, as far as the eye could see, blooming in the sun even to the reaches of the ancient church where the Camino winded, and the three of us, mother, father and daughter, embraced on the roadside with heartfelt joy, this after the hard ride. We sipped wine and broke bread in the cloister marked by the cross of St. James and it was good, this life.

Yes, maybe it was true.

Some believed wrongly that Cortez and DeSoto were Pahana, the lost white brother whose return was prophesized by the Hopi. Their brother's return heralded the end of the fourth world and the beginning of the fifth. Pahana was prophesized to bear an emblem, which these Spaniards certainly did—the yoke and bars of Ferdinand and Isabella, the red lion of Spain. Lost Brother was to bring a tablet, with the missing half of creator's words, and the fierce ones who rode on big dogs, they brought books to tally Aztec cities of silver. And Pahana was supposed to offer his empty white hand as a sign, and Cortez had done exactly so, before filling it with the flash of steel.

For a people who'd hunted and fished their way out of Africa, borne east across a vast backbone of earth, burying their dead on beds of ground ochre, surrounded by deer bone carved into hunting points, who'd traversed the great land bridge thirty-five thousand years before in pursuit of the sweet-fleshed camel and giant sloth and tusked wooly mammoth, who'd flaked the Clovis points under the living sky on a night when a sun exploded and their shadows danced crazily on the ribbon of land they named *changa luta*—the great red spirit road of this life. How the old ones, the shadow-shamans who passed ten thousand moons before the basket makers, the ones who'd brought stone to life and turned them red with holy ghost panels that served as spirit portals, outside to inside, diamonds on pottery shards in Chinle Wash where quartz from Arkansas had flowed east to west before even the twenty-nine floodings, when the land was under the ocean of the third world, when the terrible *wakan* lizards whose backbones cropped up on buttes the Cheyenne hold sacred, who were they to know the difference?

Some trusted the Spanish with their sail-furled galleons. They bore the insignia of Pahana, held before them open hands of shimmering white. Lost White Brother had come to them from the big waters and a better world was at hand.

It would not be.

The peoples' blood rained blood-red poppies and it was not so. Cortez the killer—he was not Pahana.

Nor DeSoto. Still, from Spain they came. The old world had reached out to the new. The bridge was built. It was no dream.

In Peru, there had been a thin-waisted princess, an Inca whose father had slit her throat outside a wide stone room that shone with gold from the floor to the ceiling. Her eyes were slate-colored, and shone out at the men who carried silver around the corpse for two full days, afraid to touch her. The eyes stared at them, one and then the other, and made them homesick for all they had loved and left behind. On her, the men smelled their former lives, the warmth of lips to kiss and murmur the sounds of love. A lord's daughter, he'd been right to slit her throat, better that than the other. She'd gushed into the roomful of precious metal; her eyes *knew* and *knew* and *knew* the men as none before or after. In a spring flood, Don Hernando saw the princess's eyes again and knew them for what they were, the power of their slate-colored hold. The eyes seemed a passageway, adrift, this Inca princess with the thin waist whose father had slit her throat. She came to Hernando on the eve of his death, and her eyes were not without pity.

"Don Hernando, have I not pressed these lips to your own on the hyacinth veranda near Cadiz? Have we not shared blood and wine and water? Love? Will you not take me?"

Even as he drowned, Don Hernando was buoyed. Gulping breathfuls of river, he kept saying *yes. Yes.* The final thought, *yes. Love.*

He died on May 21, lost in an unknown land.

1542 coincided with the fourteen-year floods on the big river the natives called *Tamaliseu, Tapatu,* and sometimes *Mico or Ri.* So that the Indians would not find a corpse to undo their belief, De Soto was eviscerated, the gut cavity sewn full of river rocks. They oiled the body, dressed it in the finest suit of Incan silver. The metal reflected bits of starlight as they ferried him out into the flood. Don Hernando de Soto lay on his back, ever to gaze up through muddy waters. On clear days, the buzzards see a fierce shining, how it catches the blood-red sun, offers it up to the fathomless sky.

El Camino and the Red Road—they converge on the Blue Road of this life, where we drank wine, broke bread and cheese in the cloister of the church in the field of red poppies, where our lives stopped and started and we were three peregrinos in another country, on another continent, taking sustenance beneath the cross of St. James. On an afternoon when we seized life and were seized, I have not forgotten that.

4.

Saintly Ramon drives us the last of it to Burgos, where lay the body of El Cid. The bus smells of us now, reeks, bike socks and soaked shirts, the mean-hearted bike pants with their stinking butt pads, all strung from the backs of seats as we roll into the first real deal city since Madrid, wherein resided Ferdinand and Isabella when Christopher Columbus was received in 1497, bearing with him the golden chariot of Moctezuma, which they now had paraded around the city on Easter Sunday, driven by a cardinal, his red snake tongue of a hat shining. I'd brought tobacco, good hand rolling stuff without additives. It was in Burgos that I first smoked openly in front of the group, just rolled one up bus-side at the take out in front of our hotel where it was desolate and grey and there was a big wall you had to walk through to get to the thoroughfare where there was a canal, or maybe it was a hedge, I don't really remember, only we rushed like hell, the three of us, to hump our bags up the stairs, faster than the elevators in Spain, we'd learned, showered the stink off our bodies in a frenzy, the little Spanish soaps strange smelling under the hot water. We met Christoph and Fernando on the sidewalk where we walk, walk, walked to the dark cathedral where we'd end our day at the foot of Rodrigo Diaz de Campeador who the Moors called Lord, El Cid, epic hero of Spain whose story—and horse, Biebeca, even—are known by every school child from Navarre to Galacia, having read and memorized *"El Cantar de mio Cid"*, the very genesis of Iberian poetry in 3700 verses which I'd been asked to present tomorrow for dinner at Carrion de Conde, the ancient homeland of the Cid's enemies.

I laid tobacco at the grave, a pinch, and as always, Ray sifted a sprinkle in a corner overseen by a half-dozen cardinal hats where was *Capilla de Santa Tecla* with its rococo ceiling, martyrs and retablo retelling the birth of Christ, sculpted by the god of the stone world, Gil de Siloe, the young Mary seated on her mother's lap, learning to read. Our tour guide assures us all these rooms, these chapels, are cram-packed with dead people who've bought the right to be buried in the Cathedral with El Cid and Doña Jimena. Within a rock's throw of *Capilla del Santo Cristo de Burgos,* the chapel of the Black Jesus who was found floating in the sea possessing very real fingernails, a crown of thorns, hair, blood, bone and skin, so that the relic must be shaved each day. So the headset said, the one that directed us place to place, though mine had a whistle in it, and the woman's voice would suddenly switch from English to French to Spanish and then silence, whale song from the deep's heart.

We all carried somewhere on our person the *Ano de la Fe, Credencial del Peregrino*, a many-folded booklet with colorful stamps verifying where we'd passed, from Jakue in Puente la Reina through Navarra to Santa Domingo del la Calzada with its bold blue chicken juxtaposed above the cathedral, tree, and gothic spire, to Burgos, Santa Iglesia Catedral, twin spires above the scallop shell, fecha 27/6/13. On the *Ano's* face, gloriously rendered in Italian marble, a robed woman holds a cross in one hand and chalice in the other, blindfold, as she has not lived to see the birth of Christ, but has faith for the next world who will surely see.

The next morning, day three on the Camino, butt-sore for sure and feeling the miles, we detoured around a hill like death, a wide circle that swung our cycling line through farmland and a sign not remotely close to anywhere at all announcing the place as *Matajudios,* place where the Jews were killed. Fernando shrugged and we kept on pedaling the twenty miles that would get us to Ramon. Lyra had been awarded the turtle jersey, our relic, awarded to Ron and NiNi by an Aussie who'd ridden with them from St. Petersburg to Paris, and was now bestowed from one of us to the other at dinner, washed furiously in a sink with powdered soap, then almost dried on an overnight line, passed on before first light when we hurried to dress and get on with it. Past *Castrillo de Matajudios* we crossed the river Pisuerga, the death hill far away now, and the shirt of the turtle had given my daughter strength, now that the land had flattened and wild flowers grew across uncultivated farmland—Lyra simply flew, her Rockhopper up far ahead with Fernando and Merrilee, Ray and Liz, real cyclists. Jill and I stopped once for water and when we looked up everyone was gone.

In affliction is redemption.

True Heart had told Nicki Davis this before she sundanced the last time, when Kurt had asked me to assist him at the south gate where flesh offerings were given and taken. With a very real razorblade he'd slice pieces of skin pricked up with a pin on the donor's bicep, place it in a square of red cloth in my hand. He'd talk while he was doing it, tell jokes, shoot the shit, and each time they walked away, blood curling down their wrists and hands, he'd have me burn cedar and I could tell that it was hard for him, that this flesh taking was heavy business.

In affliction is redemption.

Who knows why I thought of that there stopped with Jill on the road, drinking our hot water. I don't remember if we talked, but we were surely afflicted, on the flat road beside the field of wild flowers. Lyra had ridden away from us in the turtle shirt with adults, and it was maybe the first time anything like that had ever happened, for her to leave us that way.

Christoph disappeared and reappeared in Fromista carrying these giant paper sacks stuffed with deli sandwiches, good cold cuts and cheese and lettuce and tomato that we scarfed down in a park next to a leather shop where NiNi bought a real expensive purse and Jill decided she'd had goddamn enough, and that we would not ride the additional 50 kilometers to *Carrion de los Condes*. We'd take the bus with Ramon, NiNi and Ron and tour a Roman villa, which was fine by me and Lyra.

Twenty kilometers north of *Carrion de los Condes*, on a verdant plain not so different from the Mississippi Delta country of my childhood, at a place so flat and remote that the countryside loses us and we shut eyes and let sleep come, we arrived at *de la villa Romana del la Olmeda*, where in 1968 a farmer's plow blade struck something solid, so he started digging and what he exposed made his heart beat hard in his chest so that he had to sit down, cover his eyes and breathe, and even then the image would not release him from its grip.

There was a parking lot, a vast metal building with windows and scaffolding, and inside a place to buy tickets, take a pee and fill water bottles, clamp on the headset and walk through the glass doors into a bright room, the size of a football field, maybe bigger, with raised walks winding through tile mosaics crafted by Roman artisans, slaves likely, of a sort and quality and fierce beauty as to—yes—make the heart beat hard and take breath away.

Here had been a fortified villa, a compound situated in prime farm country where the hundreds of slaves cultivated the land, brought forth wine and cheese and meat and the fruit trees hung heavy for the reaping. The Romans had come for gold, built their cantilevered roads we'd ridden from the poison river onward, and it had been on a Roman road that we last saw Bill before the first miracle of the Camino. The graceful arches and domes of Romanesque architecture had followed us along the way, and we'd encountered the occasional artifact—the metal works in Toledo, bath houses, a column sculpted as if alone, the afternoon sun prismatic in its cornice and frieze. Roman mines had been marked over the Camino in the guide written by the priest mystic—they were no secrets. The Romans, their presence was very much a known, a given, at least until we walked through the double glass doors into the 4th century villa, the only remnants of which were the floors they walked upon, of a beauty so fine as to be fit for gods and myths and legends that we found there rendered. And if time is a human construct, an invented thing with little meaning in the schema of our kind, then it surely shut down there beneath the stadium lights housed on the beams above. We gazed on it then, pilgrims on the way of Saint James, we walked through the outer walls.

In a room called the *Oecus*—place of receiving—the first gallery through doors flanked by marble columns, one of the twenty-seven rooms the size of our house back home, all heated by hot water piped underground, amidst baths and four towers protecting the 3,000 square meters, and here in the room for receiving guests who'd soon be wined and dined, a mosaic set into seventeen hundred-year-old concrete recounts the legend of Ulysses and Achilles, who were once said to have dressed as women and hidden in the bedroom of a King's daughters to escape entrapment and death. Fully life-sized, gowned Achilles, auburn hair flowing in ringlets to his shoulders, is embraced by a green-clad daughter, and another with arms around a heavily muscled thigh, and another crouching at the other leg, both hands gliding up a thigh to a destination the gown covers. In one hand a shield, in another a spear, five more daughters look on. Soldiers are coming, there they are with bows and drawn swords, regal Odysseus to the side with light shining on his curling beard and broad bare chest, the folds of his dress cloth as visceral as the shirt on my back. Their eyes meet, the whites of them wide, and some thought seems to pass between them, this is it, this is the moment, and still the daughter's hands grasp and grope the carnal flesh, the manhood just within reach, and the eyes of the one whose hands slide upward, she lifts them to the half-god above.

Shall I do this? Shall I go there?

There was mirth here, the two great men in drag, caught in the bedroom of giggling girls, wide-legged and nude, the moment at hand. To be walked across and stood upon, what must they have thought to have such beneath them? How many had got on hands and knees to view the lump curving beneath Achilles's gown? Had wine spilled there and one fell to lick it from cold tile?

The colors are real, vibrant as my wife's eyes that second.

How was this possible? How on earth?

Next room over, the hunt scene lay in the dining room, one of two, and there was no humor there, but sheer bloodlust framed in the chaos of a moment when the hunted beast turns on its pursuer and draws blood. A wild boar has just gutted one of the hunt dogs circling it, there it stood wild-eyed, the bristles on its back straight up, another dog leaping through a gush of blood red blood for the attack. Heavy muscled shoulders sweat-slicked, the beast squares on the dogs, another leaping from behind now, the tusks gleaming fiercely in the lights. The hog spins to face us now like some goddamn Neolithic dragon. Magnificent, big as a bull, it snorts its way through the millennia, oblivious.

A leopard leaps onto the hind end of a horse, buries fangs in flesh so that blood spurts to the ground, the rider frantically aiming spear between the huge cat's shoulder blades. Then a lion mauls a gazelle while another is speared through the heart. Dizzied, we stumbled out along the catwalk to catch breath and water to turn away the taste of blood and bile.

Two thousand years past, they traveled here on horseback, in chariots, the barefoot slaves under heavy packs. The nobles came from Rome to escape taxation, to create for themselves kingdoms where they would be as Gods. They struck gold and one mine not twenty miles from where we stood then on the banks of imperial Rome yielded 20,000 pounds of ore in one month for the Lord of this villa under the blue skies of what thirty thousand years earlier had been an ancestral home for homo habilis or erectus or Neanderthal—the verdant plains with their giant sloths and camels and gushing berries and sweet water for the taking. The Iberian Peninsula from whence sprang the Basques, whose language was kin to none on earth, who taught the Vikings to sail west to the great Atlantic fields of cod, taught them salt and preservation, how enough meat to feed an army could be had from mother earth. They'd fought the Moors who'd sailed from Africa and built mosques and named the world. Imperial Rome, the feasts and wine—such a crossroads spins out spiraling through timeless thought. Surely this was earth's heart, buried beneath the field in summer on the Camino.

Through one window was the parking lot, Ramon visible in the driver's window. I wondered if he had a daughter, if she'd one day ply the Camino, cast eyes on wily Odysseus and half-god Achilles, dipped in the river by goddess Athena, here where myth became flesh bequeathed in stone.

We turned to face an expanse that stretched all the way to darkness. There was a field of squares divided into threes, and in one of the three squares was a swastika, the zigzag outlined in black tiles and filled with white ones in a square of red maybe two feet across, and this lay outlined in gold and then black and then white and then black. The swastika alternates with a perfect Gordian Knot, tied by Gordius, King of Phrygia, held to be capable of being untied only by the future ruler of Asia, and cut by Alexander the Great—student of Aristotle—with his sword. Alternating with this, a medicine wheel cross, more intricate than the one on Braveheart's chest as he pierced the headman at the sun dance tree on a buffalo hide, the cottonwood leaves wafting in the brute heat. Black, red, yellow and white—Uwipi colors—I see it plainly laid out there these thousand years passed, the east facing Lakota sun dance, crossed at the tree, gated west to the fire and lodge, power swastikas on either side, the eternal Gordian Knot above and below.

And then I looked up and it was light again and we left.

That night, at San Zoilo, we ate octopus cooked in its own ink. I brought out the battered University of Utah copy of *Del Cantar de el Cid*, epic hero of Spain. We'd gathered at the long table—comfortable with each other now after the pain and meals and wine, the cathedral of chickens behind us now. We were in a secluded dining hall with not so bright light in the monastery named for the Saint whose bones it housed, many bottles of wine were opened and going round, and we read the cantar out loud, Taunya Lasagna the English and Fernando Rubio the Spanish, the part where the Cid's daughters, who he loved, were married to the brother nobles of Carrion de Condes, who were cowards, who had shit themselves and hidden when the Lord's pet lion escaped, so the girls had laughed at them and the brothers had promised to provide a castle estate, fine food and drink and clothes for the noble daughters, but they did not forget, they remembered the laughter. El Cid had outfitted them splendidly, given a cherished sword won in battle to one son-in-law, and an Andalusian stallion bred from Biebeca to the other. Much coin and foods and skins full of wine for the trip, how El Campeador wept on his daughter's cheeks and gave his heartfelt love, as did the mother, Doña Jimena. How they watched their daughters weep hard tears as they disappeared over the horizon and were gone. And the brothers made toward their homeland and their hearts were crooked. They conspired the evil deed and sprung it on the girls before the first camp was even set; the daughters of El Cid the Campeador were stripped naked, beaten with the scabbard and sword of the Cid's, and left for dead. Naked, beaten and starving, no food nor water, nor a scrap of the fine clothing the Cid had dressed the party in, nothing was left for the girls, the darlings of their father's eye—oh foolish, heartless, stupid men—will not this deed follow you and yours to the end of time and beyond? brute base treachery, it will reach the Lord's ear, mother Doña Jimena, and you will one day stand face-to face-with him you have so wronged.

5.

The first rays of pale yellow sun fell on a tree in the center of the clois-
tered courtyard, an olive with shining leaf, and we looked upon it from our
open-paned window and were moved.

I said, "Jill. Lyra. I love you. Look."

Below us, the tree shone, and then we looked at each other in this airy
room that was once a monk's quarters, our cotton cords stretched from
one side to the other, strung with colorful jerseys that had dripped small
puddles on the hardwood while we slept the sleep of ones who've sipped
wine in a hall overlooking the field where Charlemagne had camped on his
way to kill Moors, where he'd dreamed the death of a hundred men in arms
and kept them from battle, so that overnight their spears had sprouted
roots and grown into the ground.

"It's beautiful," Jill said, and the light was in her eyes, the yellow flecks
like gold, and it was as if I'd been sleeping my way across Spain and had
that second awakened.

Then the light fell on Lyra, my one daughter who I loved, and I thought
of the Cid, what he'd done to the Condes, how the bodies of their kith and
kin were buried in this very house, along with the relics of Saint Zoilo, where
another of the Camino's miracles was said to have taken place, a blind man
since birth sat vigil with the bones and with the first light his sight came.

The doorway to the tree of light is heavy and beside it is a painting of a
man who gazes through time at us with the oddest expression, the tone of
the background utterly false compared with the light that meets us when
the door is opened and we step out into the square of courtyard, and the
three of us lift our faces to the tree of life.

And Lyra said, "You're right. It's beautiful."

This was a Saturday that felt like a Saturday, the warm light and field
of sunlit trees, some of which were no doubt seedlings of those the Holy
Roman Emperor of Europe had once slept under, the belief was that he'd

rise from the dead to lead in the last days. We packed suitcases and rolled them down the tall ceilinged corridors to the stone-floored foyer that led to the bus where Ramon was waiting with his sweet smile, and sadness I guessed for missing his wife and son. He took our bags and loaded them into the belly of the bus, wished us safe riding.

Lyra'd already mounted her Rockhopper, was riding circles, eights in the shade of tall trees, on a June Saturday in Carrion de los Condes, Spain.

On the way out Fernando told us the Legend of the One Hundred Virgins, how the Moors had demanded tribute from the Christians whose prayers had summoned a herd of bulls to trample the would be recipients of their womanhood.

Today we would see Leon.

After the Navarro heat and the wine fields of Rioja, the day upon day of eighty kilometer rides through fields strewn with blood-red poppies and the corpses of those who'd once walked among them, who'd breathed the fragrance of earth air before us, we rode into a village with a very old church from whence old men carried a statue of St. Peter on a flower-covered litter with skeleton keys jangling from each corner. Up one street and down the other the old men marched, followed by what seemed like the whole town's resident population, laughing and some crying and a pretty woman in red heels who carried a screaming child.

"The keys are for the gates of heaven," Jill said. "Mom would like it here."

Cannons were fired and a brilliantly-white stork leapt from the belfry tower flapping dinosaur wings, its fledgling squawking. Midday, before siesta, the old men marched the litter with the statue of St. Peter up and down the three town streets, then back through the open doors of the church, while we stood leaning against our bikes, the heat full on us then.

This time it was fireworks, and the child in the arms of the woman in heels screamed for all he was worth, and a priest limped out and placed his hand on Ron Nehring's shoulder, summoned the stroke-stricken supreme court justice into the church where we followed and watched as he was prayed over as a pilgrim on Camino to Santiago de Compostela. The priest cried real tears as he prayed, and the returning stork's shadow passed over the open doorway—the crooked cross of its wings bible black. When Ron stood, he seemed refreshed, stronger somehow, the look of serenity in his bright blue eyes. NiNi walked beside him. I'd heard her cuss him like a yard dog, scream for him to pedal up the goddamn hill, to get his shit together, to be the man. She walked beside him, and they rejoined us outside the church of St. Peter—the rock—who held the keys to heaven, these people believed.

Outside the Albergue los Templarios, we shared a picnic table with a pilgrim from the Netherlands where a new King and Queen of the House of Orange had just that week been named. He was dressed in orange, head to toe. His wife was to meet him in Santiago. The man carried a wonderful knife, sharp for bread. "She mailed it to me. Back in Burgos. It was waiting."

Lyra was wearing her bullfighter's cape over a cycling jersey. She made a horn of the knife on her head. "Horns of the bull," she said, snorted.

Out under a tree, in full sight of the Church of St. Peter, where the blazing white stork's head shone from the belfry, where just then the bell peeled one, Texas Ray had taken out the fabric, sifted ashes to the lee side of a slick-barked tree.

The Dutch man offered us bread and Christoph brought wine, Rioja Crianza, jambon serrano, a hunk of cheese.

We shared these there in the village I'd later learn was named Terradillos de los Templarios, legendary home of Jacque de Molay, head of the mystical Knights of Templar who'd once guarded the Way until their powers were feared and Molay was captured by Philip IV of France, arrested and tortured, burned upon a scaffold on an island in the river Seine, within sight of Notre Dame de Paris in March 1314. He'd lived here, this was his home. Here in this town of sweet-faced Spaniards and a stork nesting in the bell tower, where they marched the statue of St. Peter around the village and the child cried out first at the cannon and then after fireworks, where the women in their pretty dresses marched in heels, and Ron was prayed over by a weeping priest, on the day we'd see Leon.

The priest-mystic author of our guide said that we would likely enter Leon in early afternoon—true enough—that we should settle in then go rest for an hour on the benches in front of the cathedral's west facade, see the sunlight play on the sculpted spire and towers, which, as there had been a mix-up and Fernando Rubio had arranged the tour for tomorrow instead of today, we did. When the sun shone full on the rose window, we were to go inside, stand in the nave breathing in the colors of light, see it slide across the stone floor, the vast open space, and think on the medieval pilgrim, dusty from the road, how she would exalt beneath the dancing swirl of color. Come back tomorrow, clean and alert, the priest-mystic said. Fair enough. And as if this strange light had somehow got into our beings and transformed us to who we'd pretended to be all along—the whole lot of us limping and hunchbacked on the way to Santiago—we found ourselves dressed in our finest clothes, the ones we'd folded at the bottom of our packs for this very night, our hair combed out and clean, seated at a long table fully set with crystal and silver in a room of lush paintings—is that a Goya, Velasquez? Jill beside me, my good friend, we gazed deeply into each other and I remembered how we fell in love, how it had been for us when we were young and it was springtime, the whole bright world blown over with honeysuckle and daffodil. Ron is tall and NiNi beautiful—I could see them as they had once been. Ray had shed his sadness and the room was bright, a chandelier above us, I'm swearing. Fernando Rubio was joined by Lucia whose grace and blue-eyed peace contained the moment and there was music playing far off, a piano, high notes fluttering. And the food that came was what we'd always wanted, and the wine washed away all pain. That night in the palace of Leon, all was as it should be. I don't know why, but all darkness vanished. And there at the far end of the table, the frill of her evening dress gleaming white, Lyra, a woman now, engaged in a conversation I would never hear but knew. She grew up then, before our eyes.

Leon has more glass, and less stone, than any other cathedral in Spain. So the mystic-priest had told us, but there was no preparing. From the west portal, a visage of the Virgen Blanca bids welcome to her house, the branching tree of Jesse divining her lineage. There in a chapel was the Aztec chariot of gold that on Easter Sundays, says our guide, was driven down the cobblestone streets of Leon bearing cardinals, their faces hidden beneath blood-red hats. Again, we are told that behind the walls of every chapel room are the rotting bodies of the dead. "Believe me," she said, patted the wall, "there's a whole lot of dead people back there."

Jill and Lyra'd wandered off on their own, and didn't hear about behind the walls, nor did they exit the room with me and walk full into the painting of Saint Agatha at the moment when her breasts were cut off. She'd refused to marry a prince, said God would be her only lover, and he'd cut her breasts off as punishment. She was now embraced as patron saint of breast cancer patients, martyrs, fire and earthquakes and eruptions of Mt. Etna. Ippolito Costa had painted her for the cathedral of Matina, but I was seeing her in Leon, the shocked look on her face, the upturned nipples erect in blood on the floor.

Why the hyperbole?

All along the Way flesh and blood and real hair sewn into the art—why? These were painted for men and women and children who could not read and must have pressed into their minds visual images so powerfully rendered that they would not forget, not ever, they'd be willing to fight and die and offer their coin for. This was painted, then, for my friend Terilyn, bless her, who lay under the grass in the cemetery across our street, where deer eat flowers off new graves beneath mountains where glacier lilies grow from south-facing snow banks in spring time. Her daughter, Gabrielle, would one day stand drenched in honeyed light with Lyra on our front steps on the eve of Senior prom, their hair curled, the corsages bright on the wrists, and I'd feel the pull, a mother's last regret in this life of not being able to see, and we would see for her, Jill and I. Now, light poured through the stained glass onto Agatha in the moment of her agony, the upturned nipples erect on the floor—what a jolt, that.

The stained glass drew me, scene to scene—the reds and blues, yellows and greens, and I came to recognize an artist with an eye for humor, for beauty and line, and then I turned a corner where the hats of cardinals were lashed from the ceiling, a dozen of them, and they swooped down on me as snake-headed wraiths. A raised platform hewn from what seemed to be a single tree, the choir loft with its carved seats and armrests, stalls where the deadly sins were gloriously rendered—there was a glutton with his belly in a wheelbarrow, a priest slapping the naked buttocks of a boy. There were whores and whoremongers, breasts and vagina galore, woodwork aswirl with the vices of the carnal world, the underside of the seats carved with anal bursts from the butt cheeks of those who screamed *oh sweet Jesus* into the boxful of light. As I left, the Virgin Blanca bid me farewell, and I walked from the Cathedral of Leon into the morning light of a stone courtyard, and there were Jill and Lyra and the rest of our party—waiting for me there on the courtyard, Lyra riding in circles, her tires thumping the cobblestone.

How the art had followed us—powerfully emotive and supremely passionate—men seen pissing arches, their penises unfurled, flatulent winds such as would wreck ships, flowers growing from an anus in The Garden of Earthly Delights. The fornicating ones whose lust was palpable, weeping Marys and crucified Christs with the horizontally pierced right side and crown of thorns, blood dripping down the face, and in Leon St. Agatha with her breasts sliced off, and the nipples that would haunt me for the rest of my life, I was sure, the image seared.

It followed me.

Beneath the ocean of sky, it dogged me across the flats to a bridge at Hospital de Orbigo where, in 1434, a Jacobian Holy Year, Suero de Quinoñes took on the whole of Europe for two weeks of jousting, breaking three hundred lances and besting the nobility of the known world. We stopped there for cold beer and lunch at a park in the city where two old women had fallen asleep leaning on each other, so pilgrims took their picture with the famous bridge of jousts in the background. Christoph again brought us food and we ate because we were hungry, and before we rode off, far away on the other side of the bridge, treading the sparking water, I saw him. The thorn crown was clear enough through the distance, the dragging cross. He was not alone. Before him walked blindfolded prophets with leather straps they'd every so often slap the shit out of themselves with like the strange heyoka with his throat slit-scarred at Sundance. Now, the lot of them made a ruckus, leather splatting bare flesh, the *thunka-thunk* when the cross's butt dropped to cobblestone.

Jesus was coming.

6.

The road to Compostela began to climb.

We'd trained for this, Jill, Lyra and me, those Sundays we'd ride up Emigration Canyon, pedal the five burning miles from the canyon mouth, so we'd worked ourselves into half-ass cycling shape—good enough to make a go nonstop—and on the last ride, the week before we flew to Spain, Jill had burst into tears at the top, and we'd thrown our bikes down and hugged each other overlooking the cold blue reservoir below, and it was real, we were by god doing this. But pedaling five miles on a low-grade pitch with cold water and a Sunday roaster on the backyard smoker was not what we found on Day 5 of the Camino de Santiago. The Rockhoppers had ten gears, each within three primary settings, so one, the lowest and easiest for uphill became, after a point, unbearable for the Gills—*who don't like hills*, the saying went. Even off the bike and walking Monte Irago, the 1,504 meters to the Pass of Foncebadon and *Cruz de Fierro*, just got to be too goddamn much, so Janine and Bill, Jill, Lyra and me, we couldn't go another inch. Jill's face red like it had been at the shaded water room that saved our lives, and I thought we'd die there right that second, not for the first or last time. We'd given it our best swing, even loaded our pockets with rocks signifying the weights of life's burdens, sin maybe, though Indians have no word for that. And it was then, when we couldn't go another inch, that Ramon drove up behind us, cruised to a stop on the side of the road that overlooked the red Camino where old men in packs were collapsed under skinny trees. Saintly Ramon loaded our bikes underneath and we took our seats, the air-conditioner full on, and he drove us to *Cruz de Fierro*, where pilgrims had made a mountain of rocks near the summit, and from the pile's center rose a spire, and on top of that a cross that marked the end of our climb, the place to lay down the burdens borne across the ocean of this lifetime.

Sixth miracle of the Camino.

Before the Romans, the Celts marked this mountain pass with piled stones—cairns, and the cross is just another symbol layered upon a symbol by those who'd tread this path before there was a word for path, when the thought was an act not yet scripted by tongues. From there we could see snow, the mountains of Galacia shining east to the sea. Lyra and I climbed the stone mound together. I didn't know what she carried nor she me. From the pocket of the sweated through shorts, I removed it, Mama's handwriting was still there, the cursive message bold still—a graphic of the U.S. with Arkansas bolded, her name, the one I'd only backed out of giving Lyra out of fear that it might bring her Mama's luck, the Treadwell tendency toward the grand theater of absurd accidents beyond belief, the card says Jacquelyn, Mama's name, the address of her Little Rock office: 1509 West 7th Street, her phone number, her fax, Support Services Manager—flipped to the backside, *I love you, Mike.*

Affixed to the cross are many thousands of such bundles, hauled across the seas of lifetimes. I have brought my mother, who I love, who I miss, who I carry in my heart, who is dead. I secure it so the sun shines full of the letters that were her name. Lyra is beside me. She sees, though I will never know what burden she has heaved out of her fifteen years. She holds my hand, Jill with one hand shielding her eyes below as if in salute. Ray sprinkles his son's ashes at the base of the cross so near earth's end. A medicine wheel shines from the Cruz de Fierro, Uwipi colors: black, red, yellow, white. We leave them there together—Mama, the medicine wheel, Lyra's burden—at what I'll learn is the pivotal climb on pilgrimage.

Why have we come here to do this thing?

I don't think any of us knows, or if there even is a reason. We miss something, and we walk to find it, and in that walking, that great seeking, we relive the possibility that drove our ancestors to hunt and fish their ways out of Africa, to walk across the great land mass toward sunset, some of them, and toward sunrise, others. Across the Bering Strait and down into the Americas we came, we followed the woolly mammoth, killed him with stone points, and gave thanks to the great good spirit of life-giving earth. We laced wildflower into the hair of loved ones when they died, we sent food with them for the voyage, who can know why? I don't. We walked down to Tierra de Fuego, we walked to this place, and we set up a tree of life so that it grew out of the burdens that were beyond our capacity. We prayed to serpents before they shed skin. We worshiped the sun, Venus, Polaris, the pole star because it was *wakan* and did not move, the great earth mother, the virgin birth, Jesus, Tunkasila, wrapped in colorful fabric and affixed to the tree of life, the tapestry of this life. Abraham, Mohammed, Iktome's lair in the Hopi salt mines, the whole nine yards sundancing round the tree of life atop the stone burdens of our weary kind, the downhearted, the just and the penitent—what more to this life then when we lay down the burdens of our flesh and walk free?

With affliction comes redemption.

By noon, Ramon had us over the pass and we made a valiant go at Villa-franca del Bierzo, our last night before riding into Santiago and the end of our journey together. The afternoon was hot, very much so, and there was neither tree nor rock for shade. We rode past clumps of pilgrims who'd lain down their staffs beside the Camino and made shelter from the sun with their backpacks. Their faces were burned and their lips cracked, and we passed more than one that was crying and being comforted by another who was crying. The climb was steady, not terribly steep like the path to *Cruz de Fierro*, but steady. Lucia took to Lyra straight away, and the two had ridden together for fifteen miles or so—steady uphill. We'd stopped at a tin statue of Santiago where Christoph had unfurled the University of Utah flag and had a footsore pilgrim take a group shot, so the image would cross the sea that very night when he sipped German beer and posted our day up on the blog where our loved ones followed us. Overnight, Lucia'd been gifted the turtle jersey, and it was too big for her and she only wore it out of grace, which she showed in abundance, her blue eyes fierce but kind, that's how it seemed to me when she rode with Lyra in the shirt that didn't fit and never complained, though she wasn't the cyclist Fernando was, and it was hard for her on this the first day of her pilgrimage.

So it was in this way, in the heat of the afternoon, on the last day of June, our tenth day in Spain and fifth on Camino, twenty-five miles into the day's ride, that we found our defining moment. The way had narrowed and was hard pack with dips and rises. Pilgrims spun around and glared at the sound of our approach. The gravel was loose here and there, so the mountain bike tires slid this way and that and we'd all wrecked more than once. Pedal a bike uphill, do it for a while, say three hours in the heat when the lactic acid in your calves and thighs accumulates and burns like fire, and still the hill is there, it won't go away, and there's your wife and daughter who you love and they are hurting, crying even, and the hill and the bloody heat keeps on coming. The miles behind us have accrued, so the weariness is deep, and pedaling, even in the lowest gear, becomes an act that takes place solely in the mind. The body said stop this insanity, and the mind partly agreed, but there were others, and we'd become each other's support.

Poor Janine had lost her chain four times every day. Bill's face was burnt bright red with blisters oozing from his forehead where the helmet rubbed. Ron and NiNi had long since taken to the bus for good. Christoph ran sweep, behind Lucia and Lyra who'd got leg cramps and drank all her water. Jill was behind me—she'd found her strength, the inner-focus that had sustained her when she swam for the University of Maryland, a backstroker with a furious spin-flip, she was behind me, and the Camino narrowed to a goat trail. We were hurting. My heart beat hard in my neck, I could feel it, I was overheating, and I knew what heatstroke felt like because it got me once, and I thought about that time, when Steve had been killed in a car wreck, how it killed Mama, and she'd had his State Championship football picture encased on his tombstone, silver granite, and I camped out at the family cemetery the summer after and set concrete blocks around his grave, mixed mud with pond water and troweled each stone into place, paint-brushed the seams so they fit into his stone, his blue eyes and smiling face, and him dead under that ground, and how it felt to be me then, the living one, what can you do? And I busted my ass and made it plumb and clean and the sun got to me and they found me out under the huge oak people'd stand under if a rain came, or to escape the sun after the singing and grief. I never remembered a bit of it, but I pictured myself there on the ground with my people all around, not far from the Solgahatchia Bottoms, Treadwell country on the Trail of Tears, where the oldest of my line had walked down from Henry County, Tennessee. All of this came to me with my heart about to burst, the onset of stroke.

Jill shadowing me.

Our hearts on fire.

Then there were trees, a cool grove with a wide wedge of shade, and there were Christoph and Merrilee and Kelvin and Taunya Lasagna, lain out on green grass in the good shade. When Lyra rode in she burst into tears, threw her bike down and kicked it, then kicked it again, walked away from us and lay down weeping.

Lucia went to her then, kneeled beside her, and I could hear her talking, saying words, and there was not one thing in the world that Jill or I could do but watch this good woman minister to our daughter.

We lay there for a while, an hour or more, then got up, climbed on bikes, and started pedaling again, straight into the sun, uphill, the shining mountains far away. The Camino widened on a treeless hillside, so the eye could see an ocean of sky, a panorama—the earth opened before us, and the road rose up and strength came to the lot of us, we were close now, close to Santiago de Compostela, the field of stars. The pilgrimage of Santiago became real to us then. I believed. Energy came.

Lyra powered up the hill behind me, she'd made it through and the good fire was on her now, she passed Jill, riding hard behind me.

I heard it before I saw.

Ahead, far above, a shelter and the clear sound of ice clinking in a glass pitcher. What is it like to be at the end, the very end, when you are truly at your last conscious thought, and to feel the holy ghost fire and the sound of ice tinkling against glass?

It was a lemonade stand.

In the middle of goddamn nowhere, when no way in hell could anybody have predicted, a lemonade stand with real ice and cups and strawberries cut up on ice, and a bearded man ladling it into cups, two of which he handed me at once and I thought I'd fall down and die in disbelief. He refused coin.

Para peregrinos, he said, smiled wide, and there was a whole slew of us downing the fresh-squeezed juice of real Spanish lemon, iced with water. I could see Lyra coming, riding strong, and grabbed two cups for her and she saw me and smiled. Jill joined us. We found shade in the lee of a barn where the two men lived, and were provided state funds to take care of pilgrims who reached the hilltop outside of Villafranca. The second man, shirtless, appeared with a huge silver bowl into which he shredded a head of lettuce, pitched fistfuls of garbanzos and sprouts, tomato and cucumber, a bowlful of bow tie pasta, and then he grated cheese.

Eat, he said, *comen.* He held his hands out, turned face to the sky. *Eat!* he said a third time, and we did, to this good man's everlasting applause, *nosotros caminos.*

That afternoon, on the pool veranda on a foothill of Villafranca del Bierzo, Merrilee told me about her brother who was a poet and had once ridden a horse from Salt Lake to the sea. The only time we'd talked on the whole trip, the whole of the way from back in Madrid, at the Prada where the Velasquez had gazed us through, to Puente la Reina, Burgos, Leon to that moment, the only time we'd spoken was once when lost in the woods above some nameless city when she'd asked, "Do you have toilet paper?"

"What for?" I asked.

"To wipe my butt," she said.

Our first words.

Now, bound by the days, the sixteen of us felt that kinship that comes from common struggle, sweat, blood and bone, this dance of pilgrimage. Lyra and I had swum in the beautifully chilled pool, snow clad mountains way off where the sun was sinking, and we were to dine our last night on the road at a vineyard where another grand Spanish meal and several cases of local wine were waiting, and we knew that tomorrow we'd reach the destination, and that the road we'd ridden was a destination of its own, the room of healing shade, the brute hill, ice tinkling in the lemonade on the miracle hilltop. Tables overlooked the terraces where trellised vineyards went forever across the fields of green going gold. NiNi and Ron drank vodka tonics at another table and sunburned Bill was having wine at another. Jill and Lyra were up in the room dressing or napping, I didn't know, but it was a good time, a good time to be alive, invigorated by effort.

She said her brother studied novels, but that he did not write them. "He reminds me of you," Merrilee said. "Or you him. Which way should it be?"

There was an indoor pool and an outdoor, and the family on the inside of the glass walls made a terrific splash, so the windows fogged and we could hear them calling each other names in Spanish.

"What novels?"

"Saddlebags full of them—he carried them to the sea and threw them in one by one."

Her eyes were blue, she was very pretty, tall with dark hair down her back, a strong chin and fine bones, she'd ridden professionally, and it was all any of us could do to keep her in sight. She attacked hills, annihilated the flats.

"I don't know which ones."

There was some confusion about what time we left for the vineyard. Fernando had hurt his back and was who knows where with Lucia, Janine was in her room in bed asleep, Christoph and Taunya Lasagna were in the bar inside watching soccer with Ray and Liz and Ramon. My hair was wet from swimming, and I'd rolled a cigarette.

"He's older than me. And when we were growing up he'd read me the dirty places in the Bible. *Song of Solomon.* You ever read that?"

I told her that *yes*, I had read that book.

"I'm in a class," she said. "My teacher knows you. She's going to let me write my final about the Camino."

I said, "That's good. That's a great idea."

She smiled at me and faced me fully, as if trying to see me whole, and at that instant up walked Kevin with three Spanish beers in one hand, and a plate of tapas in the other.

She looked up to greet her husband.

"Maybe I'll start this very second. Right now," she said.

7.

The day we rode into Compostela de Santiago was a Monday, the first day of July, 2013, and Ramon drove us over O Cebreiro, the highest point on the Spanish Camino, where was rumored to be kept the Holy Grail from which Christ drank wine at the last supper. There, the road narrowed so that the bus was shy by only a foot on either side from touching second story balconies, and Fernando Rubio called out *seventh miracle of the Camino* after we passed. We looked back in disbelief; how on earth had we made it through, this path, this way, this life on earth? The Holy Grail? I sat with Jill for the last of it, Lyra holding court up front with the Nehrings and Texas Ray, the bald priest laughing and Merrilee whose eyes went wide, and we turned to see the earth open before us from the shoulders of O Cebreiro across Galacia to the field of stars that ran to the sea. From there the Camino fell steeply and then gradually into Santiago de Compostela where the party would end its pilgrimage at the cathedral near the relics of the Apostle-fisherman James. There Jesus would catch up to us, he'd be dragging the heavy cross up the Roman road to the courtyard where one stood in humility before the age-darkened face of the cathedral itself, and the reward would be the doing of the thing, nothing more.

We knew our bikes, their kinks and twists and bolts, the best inflation for the Camino's varying surfaces, the gears up and down, fourteen ways of positioning one's butt bones on the seat to ease the searing pain, when to turn loose of the handle bars and when to grab hold.

"Are you ready?" Jill squeezed my hand, odd through the bike glove. "We're going to make it. Can you believe it? We're going to make it."

Lyra walked down the bus aisle toward me, bright smiling. "I love you guys," she said.

"Me, too."

Ramon turned into a hotel lot, our last staging.

"Me three," Jill said.

The three of us hugged. There were no words.

Fernando told us what to expect, the protocol for arriving in Santiago, how we must stick together on the steep ride down, how we were to be respectful and quiet and how it might feel to reach the destination, how it could be a let down if one wasn't careful, how we'd come to be a family, that he loved us. And then Christoph spoke. I still didn't know him, nor his wife Taunya Lasagna, not really, but they had a little girl they'd left with his parents in Germany, and this was the first time they'd ever been away from her. Their hearts were heavy and I understood that, how the child becomes your life. It was a bright blue hot day. Ramon had taken our bikes from the belly of the bus. Ron and NiNi shared a pump. He was limping pretty bad, and I'd heard her cuss at him, she'd simply run out of gas on this last day.

"Stay together," Fernando said. "The hill is steep, and you'll want to finish. But let's ride together for the last time."

And that was it.

Merrilee and Kevin were out of sight before I got in the saddle, as were Ray and NiNi and Liz. They vanished. The Camino was asphalted here on the steep downhill, so Jill and Lyra and I flew downhill, the city before us now, huge green trees on either side of the highway, and the omnipresent arrow, the yellow pointer we'd followed from Puente la Reina to here blurred at every crossroad.

And what was heavy, what I hadn't thought about, was the rush of looking down on the very place I had so busted my ass to get to, and there it was, and it was taking forever, despite our speed. We passed a huge bronze of Santiago overlooking the city, and Ray and Liz and maybe Merrilee and Kevin were there taking pictures of each other. Jill and I found cold water at a last *albergue* above the park where we were to rendezvous before a ceremonial ride to the center of town and the vaulted arch we'd pass through before getting our first sight of holy ground. The bronze statue overlooked a park where wound the Camino's last wild loop downhill until it became a sidewalk through downtown which was real touristy, and shops were hawking every sort of cheap plastic trinket imaginable.

So, a last wild gravel loop curved down through the park to where our bus was waiting. From the hilltop, I could see Ramon standing beside the bus, Ray and Liz, Ron and NiNi—him stooping, she straight—there was our party, we would make it. And the last thing I saw before barrel-assing down the steep gravel loop where I'd lose control and crash headfirst over the handlebars, the very last thing I saw as Jill followed my descent, was Lyra, my brave pilgrim-daughter, standing beside our bus in gleaming bike wear like some Camino goddess flown to guide us the last of the way, her face turned up toward me, seeing me clearly, a smile so sweet as to buoy me when consciousness and all feeling left, when I was as the dead will be.

This was not so long ago.

The images are fresh with me still. I am not so old and have not forgotten how it was to be just fifty and in love with life, a woman, a daughter, to have passed over the Holy Grail of hilltops and fallen down into the valley named for a field of stars where the sun drove away all shadow. To have been a pilgrim at the end of the fourth world, entering the city where in the winter of 1540, Francisco Vasquez de Coronado—in the century before the cathedral of St. Iago was built—assumed command of 230 horsemen in heavy armament, 62 foot soldiers girt with sword and shield, five priests and a thousand Tlaxcalan Indians gathered to sail to the Indies with fifteen hundred head of horse and mule and cow, to search for and claim a new Spain for the union of Ferdinand and Isabella, and the great good God Jehovah of the west. Into the city with those who bore the scallop shell and gourd, who'd walked the breadth of Spain and further, much further for some, who'd offered blood, bone and life, I wandered with these.

Our party had flown before us now, so it was just us two wounded ones, Ron, that lost look in his eye, and me, blood running from the makeshift bandage down my hip, and Christoph, behind to see us through. We walked that way, pushing our bikes down the crowded streets of Compostela. Ron and I limped, I have to tell you, but with us walked a sunburned horde, before and behind, afflicted pilgrims with eyes pale as river water.

Everyone limped. Over the last mile of cobblestone, we joined the myriad Jesuses dragging crosses, some decorated and some on wheels, a donkey pulling one, twin biker Jesuses another, the holy men who accompanied them flagellating themselves, a whole troop of sons of god, sons of men born of the virgin, making their way to the fisherman, son of thunder, all of us bleeding now, a trail spattering our collective wake. Three in the afternoon, maybe, and I was in shock and Ron Nehring was with me, and he might have been my brother, lost to the world these twenty-seven years. Wife and daughter, somewhere in front or behind, the beginning and the end.

The three of us pushed bicycles the last fifty yards. There was a man in a green kilt who played bagpipes in the shade of the stone arch entrance. The high notes soared through the passage and delivered us to the field of light before the cathedral. And when we walked onto the stone courtyard and beheld the time-worn stones of its face, the three spires rising before us with the sun full them, I forgot the flesh wound in my side.

For such a moment, there was no preparing.

I fell down and wept.

With the great loves of my life, I fell down and wept.

The fist-sized hematoma that formed above my right hip bone, where my full weight in flight impacted a stone point, bled through my bike jersey and shorts so that pilgrim and tourist alike cut me double-takes as I lay back to the cobblestone like so many others before Iago. The jolt was a shock. I woke with Ray in my face, holding up fingers, asking how many. I raised my middle one in front of his face. "One," I said, and he laughed, said something about folk from Arkansas, asked again if that college up in Fayetteville was a two or four-year joint. As always with Jill, when the Treadwell business visits and some downright godawful moment descends upon us—like the time after my first colonoscopy when I passed out in Lyra's room and hemorrhaged one third of my total blood onto her carpet so it looked like a murder had taken place there—her eyes were wide with

disbelief. Was I paralyzed? No. Would I die? No. Would this change everything that had ever happened to us up until now? Yes, sort of, not really.
What next? The Rockhopper was unharmed. I rode the bike to the bus
where Christoph had the jumbo med kit open on the parking lot ground.
The peroxide burned like hell. We hit it with Neosporin and taped a stack
of four-by-fours over the bleeding. And that was it.

Eighth miracle of the Camino.

Later, at the hotel, Ray re-bandaged and doctored me in our room,
managed to pressure-stop the blood oozing from the puncture, and offered
me a fistful of Ibuprofen which I accepted and swallowed three immediately.
I'd given all my medicine to Fernando three days before when he'd thrown
his back out during a chair jumping contest at a shady rest stop where a
red-lettered sign said *NO DEFICAR! DO NOT SHIT!*

All during our last supper, sitting next to the twin Sobrino sisters, six-foot
Spanish goddesses who'd made it big in film, I bled through my best white
shirt, and the girls, who'd been nurses before cinematographers, ripped
through three bottles of Rioja while prescribing every cure for excessive
bleeding known to Western medicine, and then started in on indigenous
remedies. Jill was very much not impressed by the Sobrino twins, nor their
concern for me which seemed real enough at the time. I covered the dripping wound with a cloth napkin and held my good wife's hand. Beside her,
Lyra was fading—it had been a day. Christoph stood at the end of the table
and proposed a toast in German and then Spanish and then English.

We lifted glasses and someone took a picture.

"Buen Camino," we said then.

Buen Camino.

Then, after the weeping and the hugging and the theatrical farewells to
the Sobrino sisters who'd be co-lecturers of a film theory class back at the
University of Utah next fall so we'd be sure to run into each other, at which
Jill glared and walked off with Lyra to the hotel and I almost followed, but
didn't. Ray led us around the corner to a bar where he laid down a credit

card for the tab. We took a tabletop, Ray and Liz, Christoph and Taunya Lasagna, and since we were all a little happy and had already many times talked about anything there was to talk about except the ashes Ray had scattered clear across Spain, though we wouldn't go there, even till the end, we ordered drinks. The pain was a long way gone—not even remotely a factor in what I felt at the table, a shared knowing of having done the thing. I'd felt that with Jill after we drove a moving truck across Highway 80 from North Carolina and ended up in Rawlings, Wyoming on the eve of Rodeo Weekend—how we were the only ones who'd ever know how we'd come west, scored the last room on Main Street where buckskinned cowboys and cowgirls galloped up and down the street on horseback firing off six-shooters with the Medicine Bow Range shining behind them. And I'd felt this closeness on the last day of a Grand Canyon float with Diamond Mountain rising up where the river went, that last night in camp when the last of the 16 day food was cooked, and all of the whiskey that remained in the dry-boxes was brought to the table, and the skin cracks and busted bones and anger—real deal down deep anger and fear and courage and betrayal and compassion—was all turned loose for something else, for having done the thing, for having passed the way together and become each others' kith and kin, *relations*, the Lakota call it. *Metakuye Oyasin*, they say, *all my relations*.

There had been a mix-up with the bartender who was sleepy and had not expected a brace of thirsty pilgrims at such an hour, already tanked by the look of us. Who knows what awful liquor got brought out in shot glasses. But we'd toasted, and toasted again, raised our glasses, saluded, and ordered again, and then Ray paid for it all and while he signed the rest stumbled off toward the hotel and bed.

Outside, the air was good and cool and there were stars out, the same ones I knew from my own backyard at home, bright Vega rising in the east, linking together the fragile lyre, most delicate and beautiful, for which our Lyra was named, which in turn joins Altair on the horizon traced back through the ecliptic to blue super giant Deneb to make the Summer Triangle. Delphinus, the fair dolphin, flies low, skimming the Veil Nebula, remnants of a supernovae 30,000 years ago—what of the human eye that lifted to such, were they my relation?

"He hung himself, you know," Ray said. "My son."

We'd walked through the corridor outside and sat on the sidewalk with our backs against the wall where the light was faint and few were passing so late.

"He was sixteen. He came home with this stack of baseball cards worth a fortune. I should have understood."

There were shadows, but it was not unpleasant sitting back to the wall outside the bar with Ray. A Texan, the sound of Mama's people was in his voice, and there was a sweet sadness about him, how he carried the cloth of ashes on his person at all times, sifting onto the earth at places that seemed to matter.

I dreaded the answer, but the question had to be asked. There was loud silence between us, the sound of insects, night birds winging rooftop to rooftop.

"Understood what?"

"What the priest had done to him. How he must have felt."

Smoke rose between us, the hand rolled tobacco I carried not as foul-smelling as the other. The day of our arrival in Santiago had stretched thin. The bandage was leaking, some pain now, and that spreading through my body to places I had not known were hurt, but were now hurting.

"I grew up Baptist."

"Me, too. Well technically Methodist. Just Baptist who can read."

"All that guilt and sorrow."

"Damn right."

I'd once laid blocks around my brother Steve's grave, spread fine pea gravel under the sun until the grave seemed polished and even then I paint-brushed the seams between my stone and his, my block to his granite. At the funeral, the preacher'd shouted, *"Oh Cain, where is thy brudder?"* because I'd been off to college and had taken up drinking and other things, and was so a backslid sinner, which in truth I was ten times over, but the square-neck Baptist preacher had no business pushing my nose into it. And though I've made peace with all that, I still carry it with me, it's part of my baggage.

I said, "I understand."

"I know you do."

We stood up then and walked uphill toward the hotel where our rooms were on the same floor. Ray asked if I'd be willing to carry what was left of his son to Finisterre, where he knew we were headed tomorrow, while the rest of our party headed on the bus to Madrid after Pilgrim's Mass in the cathedral. He said that his son loved the ocean, and that it would make sense for him to make it to the end. It was a lot to ask, he knew, but would I be willing? Could I do this for him?

Would I carry the last remains to Finisterre?

Stepping off the elevator, I missed the turn and Ray showed me the right way and said *goodnight*. And *thank you*.

Part IV

8.

On the 2nd of July in Santiago de Compostela, we walked into the holy cathedral of St. James where an odd and beautiful song came from the mouth of a crook-necked nun at the podium on the loft before us, the word *Domini* sung and repeated, the rising hinge and pivot, picked up by the congregation, by Jill and Lyra and me, so that the moment's heft turned in on itself.

The sacrament was offered.

"Can I do that?" Lyra asked.

And the three of us had taken holy communion for the first time together in our lives, in line with the throng of dirty pilgrims with blown out shoes and sunburned skin, that look Sundancers get on the third day, starved and dying for water when they are opened to the spirit world. There was the nun, the word *Domini* that rolled through the rafters, the five-hundred kilometers back to where I'd seen my first burnt peregrino collapsed on the grass outside the Alburgue Jakue in Puente la Reina.

In front of me, Lyra went to her knees, met the priest's brown eyes and I knew what he was saying to her in Spanish, the unspeakable moment of ceremonial cannibalism upon which this church was built: *take this and eat, it is my body, take this and drink, it is my blood.*

We looked the priest in the eye, opened our mouths.

From behind, Ray and Liz, Judge Nehring and NiNi. Some were weeping. Uncontrollably. Some were taking pictures. Flashbulbs going off. I thought of the cathedral with the chickens, the one where the red cardinal hats flew from the ceiling like scarlet witches, of the painting of St. Agatha, her agony. Light from the stained glass shone on the stone floor, danced and flickered, and the smell of us was palpable—a thousand pilgrims, maybe more, fresh from the road, the dirt on us. The crucified God between our lips. The precedence of the holy tree from whence hangs the son of many under father sky, above the womb of mother earth, accompanied by sundry fishermen and ruffians, the riffraff of this earth to shake the universal pillars, a cathedral built over our bones, the way the eagle lodge fire pit is constructed above the body of a very real eagle, and I myself have dug the hole, set him in place, lit the fire, taken flesh. Good God, there are many of us.

The ceremony was very real at that moment, very touching, the right thing, acts that the heart could understand. Pilgrim's Mass in the cathedral, *inipi* on summer solstice, the smell of us palpable, how the willow people are when it gets so hot that your hair burns your fingertips and embers glow like wild red eyes—the grandfathers. *Domini*, of Jesus Christ, *Tunkasila*, who mediates between earth and father sky. Mary mother of God whose face is love and grief and sacrifice profound, White Buffalo Calf Woman, virgin transformed to pure white fire. Our prayers, they fly on the backs of spirit helpers.

So we three took communion and sacrament on that day in Spain together at the end of the road for our band of pilgrims. The taste of bread and wine, body and blood was in our mouths as we stood there watching, listening, who on earth could know what would happen next, the centuries piled up behind us as this cathedral was built on top of another, and that one on another, all the way back to when the shepherd saw lights, followed them to this spot and dug. When the last pilgrim closed mouth on the host, the place erupted in song, a hallelujah that might resound through the ages of our kind.

And the thing I had heard of but not prepared for dropped from the vaulted ceiling on shining ropes that whipped down in snakelike loops held by men in white robes to the west and to the east. The Botafumeiro of Catedral de Santiago is as tall as man, made from the shining silver from Incan vaults where nobles opted to slit their daughters' throats and let them bleed on the horde of ore rather than give either over freely to the cruel Spaniards with their sharp swords and lust. Strung from the nave beam, itself hewn from a new—world tree, the Botafumeiro swung down into the arms of a red-robed cardinal of Santiago who lifted off the ornate crown and then stood there in solemn prayer so the cathedral was quiet as it is said to be in the morning when empty. We stood arm in arm, Jill, Lyra, and I, tense, the way it is when the canupa is being filled and someone calls out *Kola lecel licun* and the drum thrums into heartbeat.

The prayer was long and heavy and I looked around to see who closed eyes and who didn't, little flashes of light from the height and depth of the ramparts. The cardinal made the sign of the cross, and beside me so did Jill and then Lyra who'd never seen such a thing I don't believe.

Two priests whose eyeglasses glared joined the cardinal who set the heavy Botafumeiro lid in the hands of one and accepted a bundle the size of a bread loaf which he placed inside. He put the lid back on. All us pilgrims held our breath. I guess we held our breath. One of the fierce-eyed priests handed the cardinal a smaller bundle from which he drew forth a tool, bowed to pray again. Light passed through stained-glass, flickered on the floor. When Evangeline placed me in the grave plot of my *hanbleceya* she sang my death song and when they left me alone there on the mountain something dark passed behind my back, an animal? a dark thing.

The cardinal made fire. He held it to the appointed place on the Botafumeiro. Where he touched it was a cloud of immediate smoke that I smelled that instant—it was cedar, something like white sage, *copal* and sweet grass. *Azilia*, it would purify.

I said, *Pilo maya yelo he. Omakaiya yo.*

The Botafumeiro was yanked up of a sudden, a huddle of priests materialized grunting heavy-breathed as weight lifters as they hauled Jesus out of the white rope, and the great silver man-sized smudge arced in an enormous loop that swung from one side of the cathedral to the other, a mighty distance with smoke like a car wreck pouring from it over us, the sweet *azilia*, cleansing our foul reek. How it swung again over us and again, many pilgrims gasping and some bursting out in tears, and some staring blank-eyed as if the sun had fallen and was zig-zagging down into the ocean, and it was then that I saw him for the last time.

Jesus, he'd taken off his crown of thorns and laced on tennis shoes. He'd removed his bloody clothes. He held both hands up palms out the way

Pentecostals do before they handle snakes, the way Sundancers do after they've been pierced when they back away from the tree until the ropes pull tight, and the big Indian booms the drum and the *Tunkasila* song begins, the twirling heyoka yelping and running backwards, chief yelling *hoka ye, hoka ye.*

The stink of us vanished—light fell flittering gold motes on my empty footprint ever.

It had been sad, turning in the bicycles. I'd got to know mine, the glitch between transition gears, the seat adjustment, how the left-hand brake grabbed tighter than the right. We'd been to the pilgrim office, waited in line for the last stamp on our *Ano de la Fe*, a blue one marked 01XULL01 *XULL 2013 OFFICINA DE LA PEREGRINACION S.A.M.I CATEDRAL SANTIAGO.* We went in to see a clerk one at a time and she asked us in Spanish our names and if we'd made at least the last ten miles of the Camino of our own power. She signed my name on a vellum sheet, my Compostela, noting in Latin that I had made pilgrimage to Sancti Jacobi, that my visitation as such was for all time authenticated, and conferred upon me *Sanctae Ecclesiae Munitas.* Jail time was forgiven. My estate in eternity had risen. The sheath was signed with a flourish by someone named Segundo and embroidered with a fine tapestry overseen by a contemplative Santiago, staff in hand, barefoot beneath a halo with the recognizable Camino behind him. The Saint's shadow fell behind him so that maybe he moved west toward the scallop shell, always west, accompanied by the cross of St. James, the very one that King Phillip had painted over the heart of Velazquez with his own hand after the artist's death, thus bestowing on him the order of St. James and validating the role of artist, the highest honor in Spain. And with the look of prescient recognition the painter gazes at his audience, at me, from *Las Meninas* in the Prada to here in the footsteps where he stood offering up half a euro for a paper tube stamped with a blue cross in which to stow our Compostelas safe from damage or theft. Then we turned in the bikes beside a café bar named Labacolla where I got one last stamp and a vodka tonic in a wine glass. Ron and NiNi each took a sip, and Jill sipped long and deeply.

The guidebook priest-mystic directed us toward all sorts of retablos and frescos and carvings, absolutely the most magnificent collection since Burgos and Leon, especially the Adulterous Woman. An attendant smiles when I ask directions to her and walks me there herself. On the way we pass a *parteluz* which depicts the Tree of Jesse—the genealogy of Jesus Christ—where Mary resides above, not touched by the twining branches of original sin, and there he is, in place of Jesus, Santiago with his pilgrim staff to meet us, at his feet the toads of monstrous sin. My guide tells me this is the work of Maestro Mateo, greatest of all the old sculptors of Spain, shows me how the artist had sculpted himself on the base of the *parteluz* in the guise of a kneeling worshiper, so that University students come here to knock their heads against the kneeling Mateo in preparation for exams.

I have no words for the crypts, cupolas, dosels or eaves, for the spadanas nor monstrances, the plinths nor porticos, the gothic world vaulted in wood and stone so meant to floor the illiterate onlooker to his knees before God's grandeur. All of this is beyond me. But the woman? The Adulterous Woman? I understand her immediately. Fernando has come with me, Jill, Bill and Liz. The guide goes off in Spanish, but I already know the key. Every detail is sensuously rendered, the cloth of her robe draped low on an exquisite shoulder, the long flowing mess of her hair, the curve of her left thigh up to the darkest of touches, the white marble as soft and rippling as human flesh, the nails and cuticles of her hands lovingly carved and sanded to a shine. And in those very real feminine hands, the severed head of her lover, fetid and filthy, beheaded by her own husband who forces her to kiss it on the mouth twice a day. Merrilee wanders up, follows our gaze and smiles. "How awful," she says.

Gargoyles are so named because their hollow throats serve as waterspouts, our guidebook says, the Latin root is gargle, gurgle, gorge.

Thirty-two false gargoyles decorate the palace we pass back into Obradorio Plaza, where we climb the steep baroque steps, some of us going right, some left, beneath the image of Santiago on the cathedral face. So many hands have touched the column that bears his image that finger grooves are worn into the stone. Isabella Catalico, it is said, suffered herself to knee walk from stairway to alter rail and across the stone floor to embrace the statue of Iago, followed her husband and King, Ferdinand. We followed, if not on knees. A long line descends down into the crypt where a priest escorts you quickly through the vault and coffin wherein reside the bones of the Apostle James, as formally declared by Pope Leo XIII in 1885. Lyra had to pee. So did I. So long in the outback, the urge to step against a wall and let fly was strong.

Back above ground, just inside the huge double doors, we pilgrims from Utah—a Ute word that means place where there are mountains— gather for hugs and kisses, tears and a salty joke about the Adulterous Woman from Preacher Bill, before our dissolution. Christoph and Taunya Lasagna will lead the group back to the hotel, where luggage will be loaded on the bus that Ramon will pilot back to Madrid for the 4th of July flight across the Atlantic to the States. Fernando and Lucia would return to Oviedo, north, on the Bay of Biscay, where their two boys are in summer school. Jill, Lyra and I, we were renting a car and driving to the end of it all, Finisterre, where the Camino ends dramatically at cliffs that fall into the Atlantic Ocean. We'd stay a night there, then drive down to Portugal, per Fernando's suggestion. All wished they were going with us to the end of the world, especially Ray, the bright tears in his eyes.

"Here," he said. "*Here*."

There was silence amongst us. Jill looked at me, and I looked at her. No one talked. The chilly saint with the finger grooves now wore the hat of a wayward pilgrim who posed beside the thing for a photograph.

Liz, the sweet Utah blonde I'd watched crash into briars off a Roman Road on the day the shepherd found Bill and brewed him tea and heard the story of the lost love that so pained his heart, she stood with Ray whose glasses shone with the same light as the fierce-eyed priests who'd made the Botafumeiro into a blurry bridge above us when sunlight streamed through the stained glass and time stood still.

A Texas transplant surgeon whose son's suicide had cut him to pieces, and what flowed out was warm and the bitterness was tinged with cold guilt, he said, "Here," a third time and handed me the red cloth tied with yellow yarn.

And his part in all of this was done.

9.

Aunt Gladys died of colon cancer—so it was in my blood, my DNA—and though Mom Edie never said outright, she insinuated more than once that the youngest sister's vision had come to me, the oldest grandson of her and Marion Weldon Treadwell. I don't know why this came to me that day in July, walking away from the Cathedral of St. Iago on the field of stars, except that I'd always wondered and even dreamed what it would have been like to be there that night in the second floor on fire, the ghost-daughters dancing, their feet swishing the floor just as it fell through, on Daddy's chest, and we'd go on falling to where? There in a bed beside my one brother on the starry summer night, the wall wires blooming. Had Gladys or fate or Tunkasila or Mary or Jesus or the Tao seen this coming and so arranged our impossible Trailways Bus ride from Little Rock to Los Angeles? And now, had I been put on this pilgrimage to be the vessel that bore the dead boy home, who wielded the guilt and sorrow of the father to the stone cliff sea? Why would anyone agree to such a thing? Who did I think I was to take on such a burden, and what weight would it lay on Jill and Lyra now that we were off the Camino and finishing with a vacation? We made procession down the streets of Compostela where the Sobrino twins were waiting at the revolving glass doors of our hotel and our packed luggage was being hauled to the bus by sweet Ramon, so that I had to tell him not to take ours, that we would not be making the ride to Madrid, that this was as far as we went.

"Si," he said. "Si." And he shook my hand, then hugged me.

Christoph gave us little wrapped boxes with ceramic arrows, the yellow of the Camino, "In case you lose your way," he said. He'd once been a professional tour guide. He knew how to say goodbye.

"Thank you Christoph."

He smiled, broad-chested and sweet and fierce all at once. "And I would like one of your books when we return."

"They're dark," I said. "Hard and dark."

One of the Sobrino sisters sidled up, then the other. They touched my hematoma with fingertips, made observations in Spanish. I was still bleeding, not terribly. But it hurt through and through, the wound.

"Then I would love them," he said. "I'm German, remember?"

"Brothers Grimm, all that Black Forest stuff."

"Yes," he said, and smiled. "Stuff."

And that was his last word, walking away, laughing. We said the rest of our goodbyes until Fernando, the even-keeled Spaniard who'd seen us through, and Lucia, were the only ones left. He said words to Lyra, Jill, hugged them like he meant it. And for me, he shook my hand, said "El Cid. Watch out in Portugal. They drive like demons."

I said thank you. "You too, Lucia, for Lyra."

Her blues eyes widened. She nodded and we hugged. "Gracias," she said.

We watched the pilgrims board the bus, take their accustomed seats and wave at us. Through the glass, they were waving us goodbye one last time—Ron and NiNi, Christoph, Taunya, Janine and Bill. Merrilee and Kevin blew a kiss as the bus rolled down hill, and there was Ray in the back window, his hand held in the ancient gesture, behold, I bear no weapon.

Fernando and Lucia were a half block away, walking uphill. "Buen Camino," they yelled in unison. "*Buen Camino.*"

We answered, the three of us, with our whole hearts I believe, the dissolution of peregrinos complete now—*buen camino.* Noon, a Tuesday, the 2nd of June, we pulled our wheeled bags up the sidewalk toward the train station where we waited for our rental. Lyra's bag was polka dotted, and with each intersection the wheels banged the asphalt curb.

"How far is it to Finisterre?"

She'd tanned. Her hair had lightened. She was tall as me now, putting her back into the heavy bag. We saw three pilgrims, the scallop shells shining on their chests.

"Not far, I believe."

The sky was pale blue and the air was good and clean. I caught a whiff of what I took to be the sea when we reached a hilltop from where you could see the cathedral, way off shining. And for some reason I thought of the town with its festival for St. Peter, the white storks flapping in the belfry, my daughter all grown up in Leon, the dead boy's ashes zipped into a pocket of the pack riding on my back.

A sign on the rental car office said Closed for Lunch in English, so for the three remaining hours of siesta—from noon until three—we watched arrivals and departures of the high-speed bullet train like the one we'd ridden from Madrid to Toledo, where street vendors sold swords and the church had been filled with self-portraits of Goya. We sat on a metal bench with individual seat backs eating the chocolate Lyra had accumulated across Spain. It was good, and we'd been tempted to open one of the bottles of Rioja from Villafranca del Bierzo, only we didn't have an opener and who knew if it was legal or not. Riders would take their seats under the outdoor awning, just warm enough for a nap, and we'd get used to them and talk to them and offer them chocolate and then they'd roar off in the bullet train and a new batch would arrive and look at us shyly and then their watches which they face down. Lyra'd offer her chocolate which a few accepted and then they'd be gone, and I started wishing we could ride the bullet train off across the country anew, the scary-fast scenery flying by. People would offer us chocolate, and there'd be wine.

Twenty-two days later, on the eve of the feast for St. James, high holy day for all of Spain, less than three miles from where we sat, moving at 200 kilometers or about 125 miles per hour, twice the speed limit, carrying two-hundred passengers for the feast of Santiago, the train would derail and thousands gather at the site of the disaster where cranes hoisted crushed cars and the road was strewn with cadavers.

We could not know that then, bidding hello and goodbye to our fellows, fighting sleep and the hours of siesta. When the bullet train would fly in on a rush of warm air and little bells rang as the doors opened, and you could tell that people had purpose in what they were doing—that they were coming to Santiago for a reason. This was our thirteenth day from home. Tonight we would see Finisterre.

News of the train wreck would reach us two days after the full Thunder Moon lodge where we'd recounted the story of pilgrimage, how it had changed us, how we were not the same people. I'd pour that lodge, initiate the prayer of the four directions, the calling of the spirits, give thanks for safe passage. Jill would sit beside me, just inside the inipi door, and beside her, Lyra. The water would turn to steam when it hit the grandfather stones and our drums would boom. We'd give thanks for our lives, for the privilege of walking the good earth, for the good Red Road.

Our wounds would heal and the freshness of the Camino, how the Roman roads rattled your brains, the heat and the room of shade, the wine and the water, and I'd pass out trinkets from Earth's end. And life would go on, just like always. It would be like that painting by Breughel where Icarus's wings have melted from flying too close to the sun. The winged figure falls freely to the sea, only the gardener goes on gardening and the shepherd goes on shepherding, the shipmate ties sails to masts and no one save you in the audience notices the drowning.

News of the train wreck would go through us like a knife. Souls who'd tread the Camino in our footsteps, who'd walked with us. Five hundred miles to the feast of St. James to be met by carnage. The feast was cancelled. Everyone was encouraged to give blood. Two hundred dead or maimed.

The end of the line.

We'd pedaled the breadth of Spain, from Queen's Bridge at Puente le Reina to Santiago de Compostela with its pilgrim's mass and cathedral built over the apostle's bones, and now, in a new-smelling rental for the last of it, driven the ashes to Finisterre, where the earth fell away into the Atlantic and weary pilgrims had burned their boots for a thousand years. *Earth finished*, the word meant. And how it did. It fell down a craggy bluff where striped snail shells glittered among heaps of half-burned boots, the newest soles still smoldering. What of the way home? What about the long, long barefoot road home for those who'd walked across Spain? Still, it was the sort of act that stirred the soul, this boot-burning, a final farewell to the you you used to be. Finally, we stood on the cliff where earth ended and ocean began. The priest-mystic called it *the most significant place of pagan initiation in the known world.* May be. The salt air chill on our faces, a day in July after so much heat and sweat and, *yes*, blood even. It had rained on the way.

A cold fog came on and the two-lane highway curved along the coast through one empty village after another—not a soul on the streets, nor in the gas stations, nor bars, nor anywhere at all. People had vanished. That's how it was in Galacia then. Save us peregrinos, the place was a ghost country, which was unsettling after Compostela's crowds, the busy streets that all seemed to lead to the Cathedral.

Sea breeze ballooned the shirtsleeves of scarecrows in gardens with staked tomatoes, out of control greens and onions overlooked by stone corncribs bearing sculpted crucifixes, looking so much like burial crypts along windblown land that ran down to the sea. And I'd claimed that's exactly what they were, burial vaults like they'd seen in New Orleans, where whole families were laid to disintegrate in the ungodly heat.

The car smelled new. It had six gears. Jill had driven and it was strange for the landscape to hurtle by at sixty miles an hour after the bikes.

I said, "They look like crypts."

Jill laughed. "They're for corn," she said. "It's in the book."

"There's no corn in the gardens."

Behind us, sleepy Lyra snoozed. The radio was off, the windows down, and you could hear the swish of ocean sometimes when a curve came close.

"Trust me. There's dead people in there."

Lyra raised her head. "They are spooky, Mom."

"Corn," Jill said, and drove.

The road was empty save the lone pilgrim here and there, trudging with their sagging backpacks and serious faces, this focused look so near the end, and wine and cheese provided by the albergues and a night's sleep ahead—the orchestra of snoring fellows a comfort now.

The cape was a two-mile climb from town. After a preliminary view, outside a new wave shop that played Celtic music and sold the scallop shells for five euro apiece, after we'd gazed like everyone else out over the fog-shrouded sea, and used the stinking bathrooms that were always without toilet paper, we rented a room at the Hotel Finisterre, and I'd run the car into a concrete column in the underground parking garage. Just a scrape, I buffed it with a hotel washcloth until it all but disappeared. It would come back to haunt us. I should have parked on the street.

Back home, we always ended up at places like this. The most remote port towns with derelict beach houses and restaurants advertising smoked mullet and chowder in bread bowls, captain's platters, two for one oysters and cold beer on tap. We were butt-sore from the day upon day upon day on a mountain bikes. Lyra'd asked for fish and chips and I'd said sure. Why not? We were pretty much fried and the town had a feel about it, desolate, not what we'd expected. Now we sat at a teensy table at a fish house called *Piratas*, overlooking the bay where the tide was just then falling.

"He fished for me," the waitress said, flashing a bright smile. She was tall, lithe, and her spirit was pleasing. Her breath smelled like warm licorice.

Jill had wanted the last place, only the TV was on another of the endless futbal games that had followed them from Madrid.

"Here," she said, oozing sweet breath, "we shall cook you fish that swam today." She'd been drinking, surely.

Outside, the low tide had stranded small fishing boats so they seemed too far from the water and silly with their wooden oar blades wedged into the sand. The owner, a dark-headed Galician with bright blue eyes, no doubt the man who'd fished the Belgian waitress from the tourists and pilgrims who'd drifted to this spot, I believe he was amazed when I took a snapper from the pile, pried open the gill-slit, and sniffed.

The gills had darkened, the eyes clouded.

"Yesterday," I said. "*Pescado nadar ayer.*"

I made a flattened hand into a fish, swam it zig-zagging before his face, so Lyra grinned at me from the table, beyond her the grey sea.

"*Si.*" The owner smiled. "*Pero fresca. ¿Cocinar para tu señoritas?*"

Santiago, a fisherman. I'd grown up with fishermen, the endless 4 a.m. risings to low-keeled boats dragging line.

"Yeah, fine," I said. "*Sí.*"

The room was small, the three of us could barely fit at the table.

"It's for pirates," the waitress said. "They're small." She cast her husband a smile and brought a loaf of fragrant bread and butter, a little platter of calamari and sardines, some good cheese and glasses of wine made right there in Finisterre. "Wine of where the earth ends," she said, the bright smile and licorice breath.

We were tired. And the light was going. We'd waited all those hours outside the train station for the rental, the fated bullet train coming and going. Jill'd mailed a postcard of the yellow arrow we'd followed for five hundred miles, and Lyra'd unwrapped white chocolate from Burgos. Now, that all seemed a long way off, as the tide neared the boat with sand bound oars.

The waitress poured red into a glass for Lyra. "Some for everyone," she said. "For your toasts."

Lyra smiled and said no, sawing bread. In Leon after the cathedral there with its shining stained-glass, and paintings of Jesus and John the Baptist and the Virgin Mary, always with white doves circling above her head, she'd sipped from a glass of white, the first of her lifetime.

"What will you do?"

"What will I do?"

Jill was a captain's daughter and came of age near water, this very ocean in fact, lapping and breaking on another continent. Ray'd taken us by surprise with his request. And that I'd said yes, who knows why? I hadn't known the boy. He was nobody to me.

"Did he tell you what to do?"

We knew about ashes. Her mother, Peg, was spread on a grassy plot outside St. Sebastian's by the Sea in Florida.

"Throw it in the ocean. His son loved the ocean."

Across the room the waitress raised brows and nodded, there will be food soon.

"How much of him is left?"

I said that it was not heavy, the tiny bundle in my pack. I did not know how many ashes made a whole person. In Auschwitz, there had been a ten-foot pile. I'd read that somewhere, an inconceivable mountain of bodies.

Just then the waitress sat a platter of steaming fish and razor clams and boiled potatoes surrounded by a legion of lemon wedges and grilled onion, more of the hot bread, loose leaf lettuce and bowls of steaming soup on the tiny table.

"Gracias," Lyra said.

"That's what I said, exactly." She topped off our wines. "This is how he caught me."

From the tiny pirate bar, the husband smiled, nodded.

"My mother could not believe that I would leave beautiful Belgium for this place." She fanned a hand, so specks of dust whirled in the light before their eyes, bent down to Lyra and whispered, "Maybe someone will fish for you one day?"

"Your fish is so fresh," Jill said. "And cheap."

She straightened, the pretty waitress.

"Because you are hurt,'" she said, pointing to where the blood had seeped through my shirt. "He sends you this."

She sloshed a shot glass full from a milk jug.

"*Anise.* Taste."

She poured another for Jill who took it, sipped.

The liquor warmed my heart and the lights grew instantly brighter. Outside, the surf glowed and food was good in my stomach. I loved my wife and daughter, and it had been the right thing to bike across Spain, to be pilgrims one summer on the Camino. *Buen Camino*, I said out loud, how we'd been greeted from Puente le Reina to Compostela. Despite it all—the ghosts and deep flesh wound and signs that said *No Defacar*—all was right and good, I was sure now.

On the way out, the pirate said, "You must not forget your medicine, Señore," and passed a plastic water bottle filled with the homemade anise from the milk jug. We sat on a bench overlooking the bay while it got dark, sipping the sweet liquor, doctoring ourselves while Lyra tight roped the boardwalk and a stray dog pissed under the street light.

10.

I woke in the dark and didn't know where I was, walked to the thrown open window, a chill wind blowing over a field of moonflowers. Clothes fluttered on a line. Moonflowers, the sacred datura that blooms only at night on the Colorado Plateau down in Hopi land, a powerful hallucinogen used for visions—it will kill you wrongly dosed. The pale white flowers unfold under the full moon, all at the exact instant, and roll tight as closed fists at sunup. The clothes were pale white and flapped on the line, and there was the sound and the smell and the feel of the ocean, the peace of its breaking. From the bottom bunk, Lyra breathed. Wind whistled over tree and water, the sleeves of the white shirts beat as the wings of star men. Jill conked out the moment she hit the bed, the anise doing its work. And I'd awakened in another country and did not know where I was, the white moonflowers waving in the field where stars wove the sky into a maze that took my breath, there at the window, and I remembered October when I'd crossed the river at night and died, only the holy man brought me back.

I breathed the moonflower deep into my lungs.

The first thing is the light. How it shines off snake-backed Comb Ridge, an eighty-mile obstacle for woolly mammoth, a solitary gap between river and cliff where we lay, stone point in hand, for the ambush. Big bones rise from the ancestral slaughter, the hot blood sluicing teeth and tongue. Mule's Ear Diatreme, the ragged throat of an extinct volcano, she looms south, black and shining over fields strewn with earth's guts where garnet glints beneath the blast-furnace sun, birthstone fire ants cherish, garnet. She takes you by surprise, pregnant star woman, life-sized baseball man, overlain with a Navajo circle to steal its magic, turn eyes from canyon mouth overlooking the delta of river. A golden eagle lay dead at the foot of baseball man, time's offering. There was the field of moonflowers, sacred datura, a narcotic whiff in the salt air, and Spain for me would always be a beautiful word sung from the mouth of a crook-necked nun. There is power in remembering how time is, how what *has* happened is always affecting what *will* happen, and how what *is* happening is always haunted by the immediate presence of what *has* happened, and how what *will* happen rockets toward you, bent by the gravity of *what happened*. The vision, a breath of magnolia from home, ice cream made of snow and vanilla, how it drifts in the forks of trees before cherry blossoms.

I remembered swimming under the sunken bridge with my one-legged grandpa who stood on a submerged piling so it looked like he walked on water, jumping up and down like a naked angel, his pecker flouncing this way and that, a piece of rebar sliced my thigh in the thermocline.

The San Juan River begins on the high slopes of southwest Colorado, a stretch of alpine meadows which, when seen from a hundred miles west, resembles a man on his back with his arms crossed over his chest, and is thus called Sleeping Ute, and a Sundance is held at summer solstice where the heart would be. Ship Rock, Mule's Ear's sister throat, rears in New Mexico, marking the clean river's descent south into Navajo and then Zuni land where wolves have been allowed to live, and I once tended a Sundance fire for three blazing days when the spirit world howled with the voice of wolf. San Juan, the ancestral bloodline of Indians for forty thousand moonflowers, home of Rose Marie Yazzie whose umbilical cord and surrounding placenta are buried in the schoolyard where she now teaches, and still the Indian-eyed river meanders over what has been ocean twenty-nine distinct times over fifteen million years. Chinle Wash bears the mineral zircon from Arkansas and East Texas which insinuates it ran northwest from Dixie, a vision, a pair of ravens devouring rabbit on Ledge Rapid, where I once waded in at midnight with an Iraqi war vet who'd accidentally killed his best friend. Half plowed, I performed a healing ceremony chest deep, and asked for the river to take from this man what no longer served him in life, and the river did. Maybe that's what I was thinking on the night of no sleep, after playing out the entirety of my life, running it from beginning to end and back again. How the river had taken from that broken down man what he no longer needed.

They found me on the other side of the river. The opposite bank. I was not wet.

In the middle of the night, I'd yelled out *help*.

With headlights, they spotted me on the other side, collapsed under rocks. They untied a raft, fought the current to the ledge side, strapped a life jacket on me. They hauled me back to this life. I'd broken two ribs, the chief in a full headdress of *wambliglesca*, a holy man on a barge, he threw both arms in the air and swayed back and forth, and I was not afraid. I gave him my flashlight and he smiled, looked me in the eye. Then the barge floated back across the river to the place they'd found me, broken but dry, yelling help, *Omakiya yo*, I was yelling.

Help me, I cried. And help came.

Closing, the double-paned window squealed on its hinges. The hotel was very old, and when we walked in the owner was seated at one of the fifty tables covered with white linen that looked to have been starched and pressed. The man had smiled, waved, and went back to eating his pears, a fluted wine glass and a pitcher of water at either elbow.

"Are you okay?" Jill asked.

I could see her eyes, barely. How much we'd come through. "Yeah.

"Yeah. You?"

"Come to bed."

And that's what I did, and she was warm and smelled of bedclothes she'd worn after the long days on Camino, her sweat, the scent of her body. Her sleep was immediate, and I listened to them breathe, the fierce beauties who bookended my life.

11.

The next morning the fog had blown off and the cape rose gaunt and dark over the ocean. After cleaning the puncture wound, taking care not to touch the fist-size hematoma that had swollen above my hip, we walked in on a French couple who'd found the marmalade behind a bar counter and were slathering it over hot-buttered bread in the main dining room. The drapes were thrown full-back and the sun shined gloriously into the room so the white tablecloths hurt the eyes and the wind made silver *Vs* on the blue water of the bay.

The couple had biked from Le Puy to Finisterre, and would take the bus back to Madrid today. They'd packed their touring bikes for shipping, were leg-weary but smiling, maybe a little older than us, devouring a whole loaf of bread, bathed in the good smell of coffee and the bright light.

"We lost one of ours," I said for some reason. It seemed right. "In Estella. We waited at the wine fountain for him."

The woman smiled, her teeth smeared with marmalade.

"Did he drink too much to make a wrong turn?" The couple laughed in tandem. They looked alike, blue eyes twinkling.

"A shepherd intervened," Jill said. "We found him eating ice cream at our hotel."

They burst out laughing again, like the lost preacher and ice cream and waiting at the pilgrim's wine fountain in Estella were the funniest jokes of all time.

Lyra'd found the Cola Cao and steamed milk. Her sleepy face had tanned. I thought to remember her always like this, a girl who'd pedaled across Spain and loved Cola Cao and the seven different hams served with Spanish omelets and churros dipped in chocolate all across Spain, remnant proof of the distant time when conquistadores marveled at how Moctezuma quaffed the hot chocolate mixed with blood, guessing it was the source of his great strength. She was all I had never been, Lyra.

Jill studied the ocean. Her father'd flown a ten-foot-tall flag with this huge number 1 on it as he sailed toward port, so they'd know that it was him, flying the sign that meant *I Love You.* Had the wayward Spaniards flown such? Had their loved ones searched the horizon for the number 1?

And how did we look to the merry French couple? After so many miles on hard road, who were we to them?

"*Buen Camino,*" they said in unison.

"*Buen Camino,*" we three said back.

The scrape on the car's rear fender looked worse in the light. We packed gear into the rental, a backpack for the climbing but left the bottle of anise for housekeeping with a brief prayer that it wouldn't get them fired. Then we shared the road with pilgrims, some of whom wore dead-serious expressions and some who flashed big grins and waved, this last of it shining before them.

"Buen Camino," Jill yelled to a trio biking up the last of the long hill.

"Buen Camino!" they yelled, the three bikers.

The cape mirrored yet again the scallop shell—many paths winding around the lighthouse toward the sea, converging at a fire pit, then splitting again and disappearing entirely over the final treacherous fall. Very few, only a handful maybe in a thousand years, ever made it to the end. There were many piles of burnt boots, but when the path steepened on the rock face, they became boots that had been hurled toward water and landed randomly. When the trail disappeared, there were no boots at all.

There, where the trail thinned and fell, I told them I loved them, Jill and Lyra. They sat above the sea, a cleft in a rock that had evidence of fires and carvings and a bumper sticker with the yellow arrow pointing at the ground. They sat cross-legged there, one scarf blowing between them, white birds wheeling above in the blue-blue sky.

I climbed where the path passed between cliff and sea, into a briar thicket, steep, the trail entirely disappeared. Between cliff and sea, wet air on my face so near to the end that I could hear the slap of its finality, smell the briny rocks with their razor clams shining, the rock where it all ended, no doubt tread upon across the ages by the maddest of pilgrims, or those with the greatest burdens to unload, the threat of falling to death—by hard rock or drowning. Jill and Lyra, they watch me as tiny figurines a quarter mile from the ending, the light on their faces, and for some reason the sight of them cut me to the quick, so a sob ripped up and I thought that this must be how death is, light on the faces of those you've loved, who know your heart of hearts, who look back at you now and see you changed.

Please let me never forget this. Birds screamed. They said *help me*, I swear. He hung himself, Ray'd said. I did not know the boy's name. My brother's name was James Steven, we called him Steve. Gone these twenty-seven years now. Maybe he was a James or a Steven, the dead boy wrapped in red cloth tied with yellow ribbon.

There was the sound of the great ocean crashing into the cliffs and far across where the water flattened was the fish house where the Belgian waitress had poured Anise that smelled like breath.

A white boat that's maybe a Coast Guard vessel, if the Spanish even have such—surely they do—nosed through the breakers and faced the Cape so I'd have to wait, this was not a thing to be done in front of strangers. The surf rocked the white boat aft to stern and there was a man in the cabin with binoculars to his eyes. Far above, the white faces of Lyra and Jill, from fingernail of stone that touched sea they seek me.

Pain seared through my side when I fell, tumbled to a rock where wildflowers grew from the striped shells I'd gathered as a child when Uncle's youngest had drowned in a bathtub and Mama took us on a Greyhound from Memphis down to St. Augustine, and all the bus stations along the way had that song playing—*help me operator, give me Memphis, Tennessee.* I touched it then, just a little pressure to stop the blood.

At last the boat had eased off, rocking on a curve of sea.

In the pack was the sage bundle I'd rolled in Utah, cut from the low-growing plants beneath a mountain mahogany that overlooked the valley where my daughter was born, and so my biggest change, the miracle of life coming. I hadn't known that I was rolling ceremonial Azilia for this moment, who could have told that this moment would be? Even now it was a mystery.

Why?

The earth flattened to a curve.

A thin trail.

Finisterre.

Earth's end.

Omakiya yo.

Alone among us, I'd made it to the tip of the very end. A whale rock's head, it was grey and rough and good for the feet. Waves slapped it. The salt water went in my face and I said thank you. Jill and Lyra were gone. I could not see them anymore. Light shimmied on the water—a phenomenon called *seiche*. Due east was Boston, the Azores in between. The stone was good for the feet, basalt maybe, you could get a grip. The pack slid from my shoulders. Blood printed the red cloth of the dead son's ashes. You couldn't see it save for a waving ribbon of yellow yarn. I saw this just as the weightless bundle arced above the blue water, caught air and stilled before falling. Maybe he was a James or a Steven, a Daniel or a Marion. Maybe he was called for a thing for which there was no word, no human thought. In three years, spelunkers would discover a new species of human on the earthen floor of a cave in South Africa. The species was named *Naledi* which means *star man* in the Lesotho language. Fifteen individuals were found a mile into a lightless cave, up a massive stone block called Dragon's Back, and then down to a hidden entrance two hands widths wide. He was before fire. He buried his kin. The burials were deliberate, there had been ceremony, grief. Lost love. Star man grieved. Buried loves in protected places two million years before fire.

I saw my own blood just as the weightless bundle stilled above blue water.

Goodbye, my brother.

Why not wade in and bathe wounds in the clean salt water at the end of the world? How many pilgrims had wept and laughed and screamed *dear god* from this very rock? Surely that was the way, to leap in and swim and go on swimming—and where would one be headed exactly, so tiny, spun by the current, flailing. Where weary pilgrims had burnt their boots for a thousand years, and flung them to the sea.

12.

Ron Nehring had sent his hat, evidently a thing that no longer served, for me to discard at Finisterre, only I forgot, and did not think about it until we crossed over into Portugal where no one drove under a hundred, and the miles flew by until we hit Aveiro and rented a room two blocks from the ocean on the afternoon of 3 July, our fourteenth day out. The drive had rattled us, these cars like dark blurs blowing our doors off, demons Fernando had called them, and so they were, roaring up on us so that Lyra covered her head with my flannel shirt and Jill kept saying it was scaring the pee out of her.

We carried our selves and wheeled bags up two flights of stairs, opened yet another hotel room, this one with a nice balcony with chaise lounges that faced away from the Atlantic. I've forgotten what it cost and the color of the walls and whether the bed was soft or hard.

We walked to the ocean and lay down on the sand, and went to sleep that way for a while. The warmth of it felt good on my hip and Jill lay down beside me, she smelled like dust on the Camino, when the legs burned and you breathed it in hard, mixed with poppies and sweat.

Lyra'd run off into the breakers in an orange bikini. There was a big-bellied man in a white t-shirt wading knee-deep, and three young girls who squealed, and a tanker offshore, big as an island, moving north.

We'd decided long before to extend the trip beyond Finisterre, to make a quick run down into Portugal where Fernando had recommended Aveiro as a place he loved, then double back to Madrid for the 4th of July and fly home the following day. All our clothes were dirty, mine mostly blood soaked, and Lyra'd run out of underwear. We were ready to go home. I was. All this felt like the song Merrilee had sung while pedaling on the brutal day we lost Bill—*merrily, merrily, life is but a dream.*

We needed to go home.

The hat that I remembered, Ron's, had M22 in white letters across the bill, the name of the road by their cottage in Michigan. He gave me the hat with much ceremony, as if it held the heft of the red cloth and yellow ribbon Ray had put in my hand. A supreme court chief justice from Kalamazoo, a world class 800 meter man for the Chicago Track Club, and the World Champion Ride and Tie athlete for three years running, his life was one of gigantic leaps up the ladder, and the higher you climbed up the ladder, my grandfather told my mother on the day she announced her promotion to manager, the more of your ass shows. His body'd turned against him, all he could do to get on a bike and ride. Before the hilltop of blood-red poppies, I'd hung back and heard NiNi cuss him like a yard-dog. In a year, he'd be forced to retire, and even some of the cases he'd had the deciding votes on would be reviewed. NiNi'd have me to the library of his Matheson courthouse office where his minivan sized desk shone with a casket's luster, and bookshelf after bookshelf was lined with books of a literary man: *The Complete Stories of Ernest Hemingway*, Robert Stone, Richard Ford, Wallace Stegner, Twain, *Blood Meridian*, *The Complete Book of Esquire Stories*, all the *Best Americans*, a fifteen-pound Encyclopedia of Baseball, the law journals he'd edited, he gave this to me. I don't know why. Maybe he remembered how me and Christoph had shepherded him through the stone arch where the man in the green kilt played searing bagpipes, how the face of the cathedral had shone before us and we fell down and cried. We packed a chunk of his library in banker's boxes and two-wheeled it all down to my truck, and that was that. NiNi'd been late, and I'd had to loiter in the courthouse lobby where I could tell the guard cops were staring at me, that they knew I'd never been in a courthouse without the fear of jail, how many times I'd tasted my own bile in courthouses, and never had I been there one time for anything remotely pleasant.

"You're such a strange man," she'd told me, leading me to her husband who had a hundred-dollar bill crumpling out of one pocket of a tattered coat.

And a year after that, she'd fall in love with a man from Boulder. Ron would go to assisted living in Salt Lake where he could have a dog and someone to cook for him and button his shirts. The *gulag*, he called it. M22 was the name of the vacation cottage they'd shared on a Michigan lake during forty-one years of marriage. It had sold that year. The heft of their life in love.

I didn't know all this then, on the afternoon in Portugal, when my daughter skipped through the waves in an orange bikini, motioned me to join her, which I did, but not before frizbeeing the M22 hat as far out into the ocean as I could throw it, only not far enough. The surf rode it back to me. I threw it again, the *ta, ta, ta* of it winging away, riding the surf back to where I stood. Lyra stood glistening with sand on her face the last time, when she picked the hat up, wore it backward on her head, walked off down the beach and pitched it in herself.

So it was done.

Back in Madrid for the next day flight home, the 4th of July weekend had coincided with the most elaborate Gay Pride March in the history of Spain, and so our arrival and subsequent last happy hour at the pool of Hotel Mu-cure Santo Domingo commenced amongst the great thrumming coalition of the queer new world. The rooftop pool overlooked Madrid. Vines and hanging gardens of blooming flowers and fern and fruit cascaded down the floors into the shade of cavernous balconies. We could see the hundred green acres surrounding the presidential palace where quail and pheas-ant and ring-necked dove were kept for blood sport. There was the square where a bronze of Lorca stood and the band of gypsies had cavorted upon us with tapas and wine, the very doorway to Don Quixote's angry wind-mills and the place where men dressed as bulls had marched in protest. On this rooftop a pair of bartenders mixed beach drinks and martini tumblers, gin fizzes and tequila sunrises, every sort of margarita known on earth, doubles and triples in the glass goblets. From this high vantage could be seen the Camino de Santiago, a vein of which runs north and west from whence we've gone and come again.

We had a booth.

What you could call a booth. A table up against the rail. Sixteen stories high with sailcloth-covered chairs. The table was glass and the floor was tile, Italian buff up to the pool's lip. The water was pale blue and cold by the look of it, every square foot inhabited by near naked men.

Lyra stared out at them, and then at me, and then back at them.

There were hundreds. They were legion. Surely the rooftop was far beyond what code allowed. Surely this rooftop would collapse any second and be swallowed whole by the earth below.

"They're beautiful," Jill said, and hid her smile behind a terry cloth towel. She said, "God."

She and Lyra sat on either side of me. On the other side was the only other straight couple on this isle of iniquity, for that was surely what it was, winding up and up from the stories below, this long purgatory of stairways because, as I have not forgotten, the elevator had broken, and the whole throng of us on top of the Hotel Mercure Santo Domingo that weekend of Gay Pride March had trudged up sixteen flights of stairs to get there.

We shared a quadruple double vodka tonic—a fifteen-euro drink. Lyra's was virgin, though ordering that in and of itself from the frenzied bartenders had reduced me to a crazed pantomime that turned the collective gaze upon me, if only for a second. Tomorrow, we'd fly home. And there is something about the proximity of turning homeward that makes a moment poignant.

They were short, tall, Spanish, skinny, British, muscle-bound, tattooed, shaved-headed, bearded, wore red Speedos tight against that part of them that was thought by the Conquistadors of Spain, amazed at how Montezuma quaffed the hot cocoa drink mixed with blood by the gallon, to be a moveable appendage, something of a third hand, by those under the power of New World chocolate. They swam in circles, reclined, hugged, French kissed each other, burst glasses poolside, sang, danced the hoochie coo, bumping and grinding into one another, so the music got louder, Jill and Lyra tried to fight their way to the stairs, only they couldn't and came back to me and the bewildered couple who were from somewhere in England. Listening or talking was impossible now, just the bass line of the cacophony that turned to a wall of sound above us and below where men who were women who were men stripped beneath the face of the bare blue sky and would by god have their day, their day had come, be damned with the world, who to say no?

No getting away, the isle of limbic sway, above the whole of Spain, the road to the Prada where Velasquez's one eye beheld us—*who is more real now? Me? Or you?*

That night we had what we thought would be our last supper in Spain—tapas, wine, the good churros dipped in chocolate. The streets had flooded with Pride folk, and we fell in with them going who knows where, washed this way and that, the music still with them and they were dressed now, they looked like a million dollars in leotards, heels, Spanish leather, one nation under god.

Housekeeping had, for reasons we'd never know, moved a wooden baby crib into the room's odd nook, which we understood in a flash was built for that very purpose. A mobile was bracketed onto a rail—Winnie The Pooh, and it played the song from when Lyra was a babe and Jill would nurse her with one breast, and then the other, because that's how you stayed even and balanced.

Lyra said, "I want to sleep there."

"No," Jill said. "*Me.*"

She'd dropped the gate, the mattress springs let out a squeal when the two of them jumped on at once.

"Me," I threw in for some crazy reason, and joined them, the Pooh song playing, the mobile spinning in the bedroom drowned with many walls of water, a *baby crib* in there where I spilt wine and the thing collapsed. It had had enough, and we fell down together with the fishes, the blue squid spread on the ceiling above us, how they swirled in the dark light, the great thrumming coalition full-throttle again, the eve of Pride.

13.

We overslept. In the windowless cocoon, silent as vacuum, weary and sore and so ready to breathe the air of home and to walk onto familiar earth and pick fresh lettuce, gather eggs from the henhouse, make coffee and breakfast on the back patio while the ring-necked doves gathered below the birdfeeder and cooed, we lay like logs. The alarm was a strange one—Jill set it for p.m. instead of a.m., and the wake up call from the front desk never came. So we did not open our eyes until 8:27, exactly two hours and thirty-three minutes prior to the 11 a.m. flight from Madrid to JFK in New York City and home to Utah. It was the fourth of July.

"Get up," I said. "We're late."

Jill turned over. She said *shit*.

Though there was not time for showers, we showered, Jill and I did, and the water flew from the half-glassed stall onto the tile floor, and it was really slick and Jill fell down while reaching for a toothbrush. We threw bathing suits off the door hooks to be packed in the flurry ten minutes before we left the room of swimming fishes behind us with its baby crib splintered in the nook to startle some future family. We hauled ass down the flights of stairs with our pull bags whack-whacking the walls.

The sweet Spaniard who checked us out of Mercure Santo Domingo on the fourth of July, who was patient with our bill and clumsy Spanish and our red-faced insistence that she hurry the fuck up and tell us how to reach el aeropuerto, that we were by god late and had to get out, recognized in me every characteristic of the ugly American that she had ever heard of and more. I argued the cost of the pool tab, our room, that our underground parking had not been included. I said the room was painted by a drunken idiot. The alarm clock was a piece of shit.

Behind the soulful brown eyes, her dark hair was tied back. "*Lo siento,*" she said, punched the calculator.

A new party was arriving through the revolving doors, they rolled bags up behind me, heard the curse. Lyra and Jill'd retreated. They waited by the door outside of which a tall bellhop was lugging a cart full of water bottles.

I said this is not right. We had a discount. We're with the University. We had the group rate. We're running late.

"*Lo siento.*"

I said can you refigure the bill. A woman with red-red lipstick dragging a purple suitcase with a bow tied to the handle raised her brows, took three steps backward.

The kind, patient woman confronted with the ugliest of Americans on no less than the fourth of July said, "*Lo siento, mucho, señor.*"

Our car was in the underground parking lot, the right rear fender scraped from the concrete post under Hotel Finisterre. Jill gave me the look. Lyra wouldn't meet my eye.

I signed the bill.

I said *donde esta el airpuerto?*

She handed me a map. Pointed one way and then another. I heard *dereche y dias y no es difficile.*

I said *gracias.*

She said *de nada.*

It was 9:03 when I walked out the revolving door to the street where vendors sold cheap sunglasses and fresh juice with churros and t-shirts emblazoned with bulls *tienes tres cajones.*

We were under two hours.

Luggage stowed in the trunk, I screeched to the little machine stationed before the red and white bar that held us in, inserted my credit card once, twice, three times, and each time it spit it back at me, and Jill said shit, shit, shit. And I screamed son of a goddamned bitch.

And her voice came over a speaker right there, and I knew there was a camera positioned in the little machine, that she could see me that second.

She said *una minuto.*

I said *now.*

The bellhop walked around the corner. He took the credit card from my left hand, inserted it, the bar raised and he gave it back to me, shook his head and said please go now.

Which we did, in the car with six gears, we went, made rights and lefts, drove through a tunnel with signs that said Toledo. We hit a side road and screamed at each other, me and Jill, Lyra in the back seat sobbing, and I rolled the window down and asked anyone who'd listen *donde esta airpuerto*, and they'd laugh and point and we'd roar off, about to have a head-on any second. This was not how it was supposed to be. We were pilgrims, goddamnit. It wasn't fair. Later, when the shame of how I'd acted hit, I'd pray, I'd say forgive me, *Tunkasila, Omakiya yo*. But it would stay with me till even this second, how I turned loose of my humanity and validated the worst, how King Phillip's little daughter had stared at me surrounded by her attendants, the dwarf and the dog, light falling in from an unseen window. *Lo siento.*

Somehow, we made it. Found the airport, and even the rental car return, though even then there was a chain link fence between us and the actual return, so the attendant had had to walk me through a gate, and then back through it again to inspect the vehicle for damage, which there was, and which he found, and for which there was considerable paperwork, we might actually miss our flight.

So it was at 10:15 that we walked to the Air Europe counter where a clerk and then her supervisor and then her supervisor's supervisor refused to check our luggage. For international travel, a two-hour pre-boarding check in was required. We were sent to a ticketing agent who said she was sorry, that there was nothing she could do, and Lyra broke down then. She and Jill sobbed. Jill actually sank to the floor, and I said stop it.

The ticketing agent said wait. She got on the phone. She argued with someone on the other end. She hung up and redialed, talked in a low voice.

"Mr. Jills," she said.

"Gills."

"Jills."

"What."

Jill stood up. Lyra didn't.

"We can credit your tickets. There will be a charge."

I said, "How much."

She said, "One thousand euro."

Jill sobbed again.

I said, "Fine. When is the flight?"

She said, "Tomorrow morning, 6 a.m. 4 a.m. check in."

I said, "*Mucho gracias.*"

We walked through security, had our passports stamped, ate a leisurely breakfast buffet and ordered beer. Lyra was heartened. Child of my life, how I recalled hearing my own stepfather fling curses through the walls of time, how they stuck in my craw.

I said, "I love you. It's going to be okay."

My daughter, she dipped another churro in chocolate and smiled. "I know," she said. "Can we take pictures with the bull?"

Out in the airport walkway, near a shop that sold books with recipes on how to make tapas and paella and Spanish omelets, was a bull with a matador whose face was cut out, so one could stand behind and be photographed as one who taunted the great beast whose exposed balls shuddered beneath his belly, bedecked with sword and scabbard and glittering vest.

"Where will we sleep? Tonight?"

I said, "Sure, sweetie. We'll take as many as you like."

A Duty-Free store shined beyond the bull and matador cutout, oozing color-wild photos of skinny women with flowing hair spritzing themselves with perfume, lots of leather and white skin. There was liquor for sale, cigarettes, chocolate. Fake trees grew in the aisles, and I thought of the Camino, how the wild poppies had shimmied under the sun when a far off church beckoned, how the storks had flapped up out of the belfry and the statue of St. Peter was marched out on the backs of old men, how they'd prayed for Ron, keys dangling for the entrance to heaven.

"I don't know. Where will we sleep."

Truth was, at the end of it all, after the Duty Free shuttered and went dark, when we'd photographed one another in every conceivable guise with the three-testicled bull and bought and read a book with a hundred and one tapas recipes including one with squid cooked in its own ink like we'd eaten back in Carrion de Condes, when we seemed to be the only living souls save janitors left in the Madrid International Airpuerto and we felt the heft of existing in a time and place that was neither here nor there, we still didn't know—where we'd sleep.

Then Lyra pulled a blanket from her suitcase, green fleece, and her travel pillow, crashed on a bench. Jill took the one across from her and was immediately full asleep. Airports are odd places after midnight in Spain when you've missed your flight home. I drank water from a fountain, hit the bathroom, said *buenos dias* to *un policia*. Back home, the first of the cherry tomatoes were ripening, and the okra was blooming that exquisite purple and yellow. The dog, chicken, rabbit house sitter was wondering what had become of us, and Jill's father had found a picture of us on Christoph's blog, and he'd left a message on Jill's phone welcoming us home.

The Dog Days arrived.

I found my way back to my wife and daughter and lay down to sleep in the place nearest them, and we slept our last night in Spain that way in-between.

14.

Jill had found a massage chair that would give you the works for a half euro, only it had malfunctioned so each of us had our backs, our deep tissue, worked over in the waiting room for departure. In some far-off corner of the airport, on a floor near the tarmac, we could see the plane's windshield where the pilot's face mooned every now and then in prep for the cross-Atlantic flight. All around us are people who've been in Spain and now go home. There's this really pretty woman with really good looking kids who are snarky at 5 a.m., and a real handsome husband who's gone to look for coffee and can't find any, comes back so they all snark at each other. There were people conked out with silly pillows around their necks. There's a woman with a little dog on her lap. I don't recall a TV being on. And there was us, different now, fresh from Portugal and Finisterre and the cathedral where we'd taken communion together, and the crook-necked nun had sung *domini*.

We loaded onto the air bus, back and back to our seats which I don't remember except to say that we were not together. Jill and Lyra were in the middle, an aisle between us. We're not crazy about flying. In fact, we outright don't like it, have dreamed of crashes each of us, and seen the photos, imagined that last minute—it's not hard to picture that. Here, this close to going home, that fear came on me. I saw it in Jill's eyes, Lyra's. The big engines thrummed to life and the fuselage began to roil, to gather speed, and just before she took off, when we'd reached top speed and the first sliver of sun we'd follow all day shone through my window, Jill reached her hand across the aisle and I took it gratefully. Lyra grasped the other, and it was like it had been so many times before when we had stood together, when the three of us were one.

We held on that way to altitude. Then a stewardess passed out blankets and little pillows and we slept till afternoon.

The sun set.

The plane touched down.

After midnight we lay down in a Harlem hotel. Maybe the toilet overflowed. Or it was something about the door not locking. The one bed. We might have ordered pizza. Probably we ordered pizza.

The four hours in New York City we slept. All our clothes were dirty. The room smelled like us. My family. My people. In whose veins flowed everyone I had ever loved, or would ever love. We were going home.

When Lyra was a girl we'd play this game where we'd lay a blanket down in the floor of the room with many windows, call it the Darvy ship. There, we'd stow cans of ravioli and tuna, the dangling cord and receiver of a dead telephone so we could talk to Mommy while at sea, a stick with a piece of red yarn tied to it so we could catch fish, books, pillows, binoculars we'd look through backwards to make the world outside a million miles away.

"All aboard," she'd say.

We'd talk to Jill through the dead receiver and make believe she was answering, that each of us wasn't engaged in a one-way conversation. We'd pretend to eat and someone would fall overboard and get eaten by a shark and we'd cry and have a make-believe funeral and sing goodbye mate, it's been good to know you.

It seems now that the Darvy ships were always on Saturday afternoons in winter, when the easy light came through the windows and lit up her hair and her hazel eyes, and I'd think how lucky I was to be alive and have someone like this to love and be loved by. Jill's face would appear in the doorway and she'd be smiling. And that meant we'd come home, and Mommy was here to greet our return.

A long time since then.

I lay awake in Harlem for a while thinking of the Darvy ship, our game, the dream-craft traveling unknown oceans. The three of us in bed, in the dark, not knowing anything in the least about where we were or what we'd do, or how the morning's flight would be shaken by wind.

I had thought *thank you*, the best prayer.

Then the alarm went off and we rose and dressed, dragged suitcases to one last elevator, called a cab and met our flight.

There had been wind.

Not long after takeoff, Lyra to my right, Jill to my left, a wind hit us and turned the airplane, for a few moments, straight up and down. A man behind us screamed *goddamn*. Then the plane righted itself and the captain came over the intercom and told us there was turbulence, to fasten our seat belts and not to get up until the fasten seat belt light went off. We were over Pennsylvania, headed toward Ohio. On the seatback in front of me, a little screen showed our airplane making progress, flying six-hundred-some miles-per-hour at 37,000 feet.

Pretty stewardesses pushed service carts toward us, served Fresca, coffee and peanuts. Scallop shells were tied to our backpacks. Pilgrims now, *peregrinos*, we'd biked across Spain on the Camino de Santiago. We'd walked to the very end of the earth and come back.

Still holding their hands, I said the Spirit Leaving song out loud, *hoye taninyan kinajin pelo hey. Hoye taninyan kinajin pelo hey. Tunkasila to wokunze ca lena cic'u welo hey.*

The man who'd said *goddamn,* he said, "That some kind of prayer?"

Beside him, a woman said, "Please. Stop."

The little screen showed us over Nebraska, just hitting Wyoming where our first arrival west, mine and Jill's had coincided with Rodeo Weekend in Rawlins so buckskinned folk had galloped Main Street firing six-shooters in the air with the Medicine Bow Range as backdrop, and we'd known that we were west.

And then Utah.

A Ute Indian word that means *place where there are mountains.*

Our landing was a good one. The cab ride home was smooth as silk. Saturday afternoon, there was Happy Hour to come and our own beds to sleep deep into. July 6, seventeen days out, there had been wind. Silver and blue-black clouds sailed overhead. Trees shimmied and the dog looked confused. No birds, they'd all lay down. All our wind chimes had blown off the tree limbs. People walked bent over. Rocks were set on top of things: the rabbit hutch, the tarp over half a stray bale, the lid of the recycling bin. A box of tampons blew down the street, a plastic grocery bag, and the blue tarp over the chicken coop flapped like an idiot's tongue. What a wind, blown across the southwest desert, Indian Country with blue-doored hogans facing east where we'd come from, slapping up side the mountains with near hurricane force, our landing had been smooth. The sun shone through the shoulder clouds. A man chased something. The sound of it was on me. It blew the lodge roof off mid-prayer when Peg died. "That's mother," Jill said. "She's not well."

If spirits manifest themselves in wind, then on that day they bayed at us, flipped us the ghost finger, shook out the monkey paw and waved it over our heads, rode the holy ghost hog in circles, bareback bucked the moon-eyed horse. The wind blew up this real funny sign that we three laughed at. It said: STAIRS AT EITHER END OF THE HALLWAY, and had arrows pointing in both cardinal directions. The train would not wreck in Compostela Santiago for another nineteen days.

That was a world of time.

Lyra's moon would come. We'd float the Gates of Lodore and on dress up night I'd don the bloody Camino jersey and say I walked the Roman road on the way of St. James. Jesus was with us, we'd walked in his footsteps.

We'd tie the lodge blankets before a six-foot fire, my white eagle feather in the breeze above the altar, on 22 July, still two days before. Night of full Thunder Moon, we'd sing the canupa song, the sweet white sage from Bill Bolan on his way to South Dakota and Sundance at Crow Dog's Paradise in Lakota Territory, would mingle with cedar and the drums would boom, and I would once again feel like a fool to be a grown man in swimming trunks, standing on the hottest of dog days in a circle around a blazing fire. And there was Jill in a colorful skirt, her face red already, and Lyra, in the blood-red coming of age dress—come to give thanks for safe passage.

Women before men, we'd crawl through the tiny womb door, breathe in the willow warm still from day. I'd ask the fireman to shut the door, greet my relatives and welcome to the first door. Spill water on the lightning hot rocks, so steam would hit my hand before I could retrieve it, and the Four Directions song would be sung. Second door, we'd pray—and this is hard, the praying, because the people have much to say, and we have many thanks to give for helping us on Camino, for the seven miracles, for the boy's ashes, for the end of the fourth world and the beginning of the fifth. Jill's prayers are sweet breath, she gives thanks to Tunkasila, the first time I've heard the word from her mouth, she prays to Tunkasila. Lyra's a grown woman, she prays out loud in a woman's voice, strong, fierce even. My prayer is shortest, last, the heat unbearable.

Thank you.

The third door is for healing. We sing *Chunga Luta,* the Red Road. Beside me Jill rubs copal on a tunka, grandfather stone, oldest of our kind.

Fourth door sends the spirits home with our prayers on their backs. I sing the song myself, unaccompanied, but not before we drink water, pass the ladle clockwise so each can take their fill, *mini wakan,* the first medicine.

The rest of the bucket goes to the grandfathers and my hair so hot as to burn fingertips when I touch it. We make smoke with the canupa, then lean it on the altar. One by one we'd crawl out into the new life, and moonlight would shine on our skin. Each of us would sprinkle a fistful of *winchasha* on the dying fire and it would cackle and sing and ask to be fed.

Food from our feast would be arranged on a paper plate, and my one daughter, a woman now in the moonlight, would take it to the fire, set the offering on hot coals as she had when they put me on the mountain and the Mandan woman sang my death song and told me not to look at her because I was dead.

She received the name then, at my *hanbleceya, Whcazi Sutaka,* Hardy Sunflower, her Lakota name, given by a heyoka Sundancer named White Plume. The fire would accept our Sunflower's offering in the name of the Spirit Nation of the new world and be gone.

Barefoot, she'd turn away, retrace her steps through the dewy grass, and the moon would throw her shadow backwards and forwards, and she'd walk in with that knowing and join us who'd come before her for the feast.

Pila maya yelo hey.

Following the Fire Priest Home

There were lightning fires and set fires and fires that had roared to life after being walked away from, conflagrations that had killed men, were ninety-percent controlled, and one Cal Fire had named *The Beast That Gazes at Us from The North*. We sensed, but did not yet know then, that the part of our lives we'd most looked forward to was over. Lyra was grown, about to head off to college and all that meant. In two cars, we were on our way back from the Oregon Coast, where we'd stayed too long and were now weary for home. All afternoon I'd followed my wife and daughter across bridges that traversed dry rivers in a sea of burnt land. Their faces shone in the rearview. Sometimes they'd see me and flash the *I love you sign*. Jill flipped me off, grinning. The truck was silent save fire radio, a government nonstop with coordinates and current status, weather and live tactics for fighting. A fire priest preached surrounding and back-firing, the import of dew point, the threat and beauty of storm. One of those tail-end summer afternoons headed south when one thing's over and another begins.

The corridor traversed a two-lane highway through groves of redwoods, these huge trees that burst into the sky from the roadside. There was shade, too, so dense and complete I'd have to take off my sunglasses, turn on headlights, it had been like driving through an avalanche of dark, two red taillights glowing in front of me. Redwoods, groves of them, some three-thousand-years old and named for the famous people whose purchase had saved them from timber companies, they grew like hell at every curve in the road. A sign on one tree said *I lived during the time of Julius Caesar.* Another, *et tu Brute? Jesus Christ,* said a third, only somebody'd written *F-ing* in between the words.

Exiting a grove was as jarring as entering—the brutal light, twenty sudden degrees of heat, and once, just as we emerged from the dark, a helicopter whocka-whocked overhead, hauling this big-ass vat that swayed away from the direction of flight. Lyra'd pointed at it, raised both palms in the passenger window. *What's that?*

Her and her mother and her mother's mother shared hazel eyes, that flame in the afternoon when the sun shines and the earth's on fire from hell to high water. What is the sign for fire, the world burning?

I made the hand sign for pull over, an index finger twirled in the air, the river runner's lingo for eddy out. Jill knocked the crown of her head three times, everything okay.

Beside them, roadside. "What's the sign for fire?"

She said, "Why should I know."

It had been a day, and now the fire.

"I'm hungry, Dad."

I said, "Me too."

"How about this?" Jill asked, flipped me her middle finger.

It was after five. We'd driven into happy hour. The air was smoky. Where were the Rest Areas?

A squadron of trucks roared by filled with hotshots in fire suits and helmets, some with axes and shovels in hand, five-thousand of them I'd learn, humping it down dirt roads, cutting fire walls by hand, lighting backfires, killing the flare ups in the Trinity National Forest and the swath of wilderness between 101 and Highway 5 to Sacramento. Riding in the beds of pickups, they looked hungry, tired, people who could use cold beer and whiskey, a hot bath and a bed to sleep in, a bucket of ice water. The very last one in the very last truck smiled, flipped us the bird, his teeth white and even.

I said, "Looks like you've got the sign right."

"*Food,*" demanded Lyra.

We'd keep running into them, the hotshots, and every time they saw us they flipped the bird. We flipped it back. By Garberville they were everywhere.

Marijuana was legal in that part of California, so all the locals had a sensimilla joint hanging from their lips, that stoner look in their eyes like the walking dead. One played air guitar in the middle of Main Street, the big smoke roaring up behind him from the Trinity fire. I paid an Indian man eighty-seven dollars plus tax for what was surely the last motel unit in town, a screen door busted out unit with a window air-conditioner. The room smelled like vomit and sex and cigar smoke and the can of air freshener the maid'd sprayed to mask it. He had a statue of a green elephant up beside the cash register, the Indian.

"Ganesh?" I said.

He shook his head. "No. Just an elephant."

Jill returned with the key before I even got the receipt print out folded and put in my wallet. "No way. Uh huh." She handed the key to the clerk. "Ganesh?" she said.

"Yes ma'am," the clerk said, reversed the charges. He said, "My cousin. He has one room next door."

The cousin next door let me look at the room before paying. It was better, though still a smoker. The air worked and there was no vomit. We carried our gear in, mixed vodka tonics. Lyra found a baseball game on TV. The Cubs—it was their year. What on earth could happen to make it not so? Outside, firefighters smoked on tailgates. Some drank beer, water, mixed drinks with ice. Their faces were burned. None had shaved.

Pets were $25 extra so I tied our lab in a wedge of shade at the end of the motel, where there were scattered hypodermic needles and broken glass. It wasn't a good place. Bad things had happened there. I brought a bowl of water, threw in a fistful of ice cubes, said, "be a good dog," and gave her a biscuit.

"Will we be able to take 20 east tomorrow?" I asked two men drinking in the bed of a truck beside our Pathfinder.

"Uh huh," one said.

"No way," said the other.

"You'll have to drive all the way down to Oakland, hit 80 there, it's all shut down in between."

Oakland was three hundred miles. Oakland was forever.

I said, "Are you sure."

They nodded, sipped drinks. It was happy hour. We'd have to change our plans.

"Mexico, maybe. You might have to cross over." He whistled a line of "*La Cucaracha*," knocked his drink back then took a whop straight from the bottle.

I said, "I'm not driving to Mexico."

That night at dinner, one of them watched Lyra from a table where stone-faced men were putting words to the season of fire. The food was good, the freshest greens, who would have guessed? Jill wore a sundress. She'd tanned while we'd been out, and unlike me her skin took the sun well. Music, piano, came from unseen speakers, low. "In a Sentimental Mood"? A horn player Jill'd hired for our wedding twenty-five years back had played the song. Our shared steak came. Lyra's pasta. The sad-eyed man at the fire table glanced our way, Lyra's. What was he thinking?

"They're playing our song," Jill said. She lifted her glass and the three of us cheersed.

That night I slept deep, and when I woke the dog was barking. At the far end of the motel, where the glass and used hypodermics had been swept against a cinderblock wall, she sniffed the north wind, raised snout and howled.

Highway 80 was open—we didn't have to cross over.

East through the Sierra Nevada, we sped down through Sparks into the valley of the sun and the great flat plain of Humboldt Range where our story finally halted in Lovelock, that incredibly run down shabby-ass hole of a town when we could drive no more and Utah was only one state away. We ordered very bad pizza from an Indian gas station, rented our dirty hotel room on the backside of the freeway. It was hot, real real hot.

Lyra put on a movie, the one where this dead guy inhabits a younger man's body and goes back to see the woman he loves, and she recognizes him, sort of. I'd seen it six times, six different hotels. The toilet was broken, a little brochure on its tank giving the history of Lovelock, how lovers historically had their initials inscribed on a padlock, and followed the ancient Chinese custom of locking it on the endless chain in the shade near the dilapidated courthouse, throwing away the key. And so, they'd be bound forever, and what more beautiful place on earth to be bound forever in love than Lovelock, Nevada, county seat of Pershing County, established in the 1840's as a lush way station on the Humboldt Trail to California, golden California, dream of America, destiny manifest in fire.

The room was cold enough to hang meat, Jill and Lyra under a blanket.

We'd got to the point where the lovers reunite in a gym where he's walked out of a basketball game, having proved himself a star. They can't stay together, he has to give the boy his body back.

Thank god there was vodka left.

I poured one, walked outside where it was getting dark, the dog tied to a telephone pole, the lonely sound of a train wailing somewhere far off on the Humboldt Trail to California where the Beast gazed down from the north. The place was a dump. A cop lived in one of the units. He walked out under the sky shirtless, smoked. I was glad that we got out of the fire, that we hauled ass east from Oakland to here. Tomorrow we'd be home. School would start and Lyra's little bedroom next to my home office would be empty, and when I stepped down the steps in the dark and turned on the typewriter, she'd be gone. Jill'd tap the window and say *I love you* on her way out. Our thirtieth would come and go—maybe we'd travel. The stars sprayed out above me. Maniacs, they dazzled and stuttered. The air-conditioner whirred in the window. The dog was a shadow tied to a pole.

I had a friend once who was a railroad caboose man, who maybe sat at the end of that very train wailing off toward California. What had it been like for him at the end of it all, hurtling through the dark and light? Had the motion got into his heart so he could never quit moving? The dog and I had the same bad pizza gas, hang your hat on that.

I took care to lock the door. Shut the lid on the clogged-up toilet.

We're up before light, hit Paiute Indian Reservation Casino Truck Stop, where Jill filled our coffee mugs, a hot chocolate for Lyra, while I pumped gas, kicked tires, paid inside, and bought one of the cheap padlocks for sale there.

On the way out of town, before we hit Highway 80 and flew through Winnemucca and Elko toward the Salk Lake Desert and home at last, I coaxed them to follow me to the Pershing County Courthouse, where I found the chain that had no end, padlocked the silver ornament with our three initials in red cursive, and threw the key toward into bushes where no doubt lay the brother, sister and cousin keys of soulmates from across the ages, bound through space and time beneath the big sky in the eternal desert.

"There," I said.

"There," Jill said.

"I'm driving," Lyra said. "Mom, ride with dad."

We load up just like she said, hit the road one last time, our love locked.

The Iris Blooming in Front of Our House

From the study window, east facing, I have a full view of the stadium, a big silver U on either tower. On game days, this close to ground zero, the place is a circus. Or used to be, back in the Old World. Which revisits us out of the blue today. Online finals are all done, and whatever students had made it back from Spring Break—not many, President Watkins had put out the STAY HOME order early on—are now on shelter at home lock down. Kicked out of the dorms and forced to crash with friends, some of whom lived on University Street because it was party central back in the day, these students, they've *sheltered in place,* watching Netflix, eating who knows what, all those delivery pizzas with the drivers wearing shorts and whatever masks they could scrounge, rubbing hand sanitizer on blue-gloved hands, eyeing their paper money like it was evil, because it probably was. They say the virus can live on cardboard for twenty days. Truth is, you can't trust anything anymore. The mail, the fence gate, garbage bin, the soles of your shoes—it was all fair game for Covid, which I've decided puts me in the mind of covert and livid, sort of spliced together, add the 19 and *voila,* just what the doctor ordered.

Only not quite, because there's this new thing called "quarantine fatigue." Which is sort of like, lock people down, I'm talking young people in their prime with spring in their blood, say for six weeks or so, feed them delivery pizza and jelly beans leftover from Easter, and did I tell you that the liquor stores are starting to be shut down, in Moab, Murray, St. George, just a few, I know, but there's that new layer of anxiety—I'm not immune. So lock us all up with shitty food, then threaten to shut down all the liquor stores in the state, add to this the whole mess about the ten thousand ceiling fans and refrigerated trucks idling outside hospitals from here to Timbuktu, and everybody and their mother having this weird-ass dream where you're being stalked by camo-wearing peckerheads with guns, and you get what happens next, last Wednesday of April, on our street with its full view of the U of U Stadium on one side and Mt. Olivet Cemetery on the other, ground zero, the circus.

The street erupts.

Close enough to campus to hit with a rock, housefuls of what will become known as the Covid Generation pour onto the street, renters and evacuees and kids recently fired from the ski resorts with nowhere to go, folks who'd lived a month and a half in dark rent houses with clogged up toilets because the sewer system was maxed out, who'd smoked through their household stash and then ground the seeds and stems and smoked them too, vacuumed up what they could from sour carpets, and understood that they themselves were living in a vacuum, so that the world outside had ceased to mean what it had meant in January and February and the front end of March, even, when the plague was just the punch line of a party joke.

And then the earthquakes started.

As if God and Jesus and Holy Ghost just had to be sure we all got the goddamn point, earthquakes came, the first one at sunrise on 18 March, apparently having the decency to hold off on the 19th, it being Vernal Equinox and all. 5.7, the first one, a thousand some aftershocks so the ground between Great Salt Lake and University Street shook like a bowl full of Jell-O, which was the official State Food, what kind of people on this earth would choose Jell-O as their state food? We were a people who'd lived with earthquakes felt in seven Western states, who would not have lifted a brow should a plague of frogs descend upon us, followed by the Pale Rider, and a great bugle summoning the dead from their graves. The shit had hit the fan. Out of dope, liquor stores closing, school all but disappeared, the ground was perpetually unsteady beneath the feet. And the killer—in a 4.6 aftershock, the golden Angel Moroni atop the holy temple had the trumpet ripped from his lips and hurled to the ground below. He up there bewildered, for once in a hundred-fifty-years not blowing.

It was too goddamn much.

They poured from doorways off front porches in bikinis and American flag swimming trunks, bare white skin to the sun, set up beer pong tables and blared bad music from my college days: Boston, ELO, Journey. Bad even then. They don't social distance nor wear masks. The beer bongs come out and a bevy of blondes from next door dump a bottle of champagne over each other's heads and dance the hootchie coo. Forget the cops, the landlords who've been forced by the governor to let this month's rent slide, the utility people and the dog catcher. Fuck it all—the limbo since Spring Break, the shut down parks, the can't drive to the next county, and the summer ahead of them they'd no doubt be spending with parents who would not countenance such a display as was going down on Wednesday or Thursday, but pretty sure not a Friday, right at the end of March, no it was April, last day of the month. I watched the party catch its breath, the coeds dumping a second bottle of champagne over their heads, the pong game firing up, a loud afternoon and night ahead.

Jill'd call the cops. They wouldn't come.

We'd wake the next morning to vomited-on sidewalks, the streets glistening with broken beer bottles for a solid block, cups from grain alcohol punch glowing Easter egg red all the way to the law building. And Jill'd say she hated living there, it was the central disappointment of her life.

I never saw it coming. Nobody did.

And then the next thing happened.

"I want you to see this," Jill said. She led me through the house, said, "Look."

Across Fifth South, Friendship Manor, a retirement home for the elderly and disabled, stood fourteen floors facing south. In winter time its shadow covered our house for half the day. Three or four times a week, firetrucks screamed right up to the glass doors in front, followed by an ambulance out of which crawled EMTs in full protective gear pushing a silver gurney inside, and after it was all done it'd take the firemen half an hour to disinfect everything, even their shoes. They'd drive away with a skin and bone body covered with a sheet, and leave the rest to the fire boys who'd laugh, joke with each other, who'd cook the chile verde that night, spraying the soles of each others' shoes—it was something to see.

Only not today.

We walked outside and saw.

Across the street, under the good sun, stood a man with a stand-up bass that was hooked to what sounded like a good amplifier. Beside him was who turned out to be his brother, strumming what looked to be Martin guitar and just then singing into a silver mic on a stand. A heavy-set woman with a red bandanna tied in her hair played a tambourine that resonated off the tall building and across the street to us.

"Open up your windows," the woman's amplified voice said, and sure enough they did, the old folk, open up their windows. The trio moved from Dylan to Johnny Cash and "Will the Circle Be Unbroken" and "This Little Light of Mine."

Lyra clapped along with them.

People stopped and got out of their cars. The post lady sat down on the neighbor's front step. It was last day of April, six weeks into quarantine, when the double doors of Friendship Manor were thrown open.

Out they came.

Wearing masks and rubber gloves and pajamas, some of them, onto the parking lot. The trio had turned it up and launched into an old-time version of "I'll Fly Away," the gospel tune I'd had played at Mama's funeral, because she loved it, and it was hopeful and seemed right. They sang along, the elderly and infirm, some of them dancing right over the asphalt where not two days ago the fire truck and ambulance had sat waiting and they'd seen it through their blinds and knew it was coming for them, that cold gurney. For all of us. It was.

It surely was.

In the shadow of a coliseum and cemetery, they poured out of their quarantine houses and made song for the first time in many a dark day. The old folk saw us on our front porch, and the goings-on all down the street, waved for us to join, big holy smiles on their faces. Lyra crossed first,

Jill followed. Some of the people who'd pulled over left their cars right on the street, and the post lady carried over her bag of undelivered mail. They were playing "The Old Country Waltz," about living and losing and crying. With me came a host, beer ponged and champagne-drenched, the singing voices of young and old intermingling, and time came back to us for just a little while there on the glittery parking lot, buoyed by whatever draws one human being to another.

"What do you call an earthquake during a pandemic," a man I'd seen walking in the cemetery with a crooked snake stick asked through a mask.

Bright sunshine shone in his face.

Behind him stood a woman who looked for the world like my maternal grandmother, the last time I saw her at the nursing home in Lonoke. Springtime, I picked daffodils and opened her windows, turned the stifling heat off. The three of us had flown out to tell her bye, and Lyra played "For All We Know We May Never Meet Again," on an out of tune piano during early-bird supper. Mom Edie, she'd hardly known us at first. I wheeled her out on the floor and we'd danced that way, with the wheelchair, while Lyra played the old song from the musical jewelry box she'd mailed one of those far-off Christmases when yet again we didn't go home. How we'd turned in circles. Another couple joined. Voices had risen to meet the notes.

This was like that. His bright eyes twinkled.

"A Panquake," he said, laughed through the mask.

Friendship's east wing residents rose up each morning, the Oquirrhs going red across the valley, and before them was Mt. Olivet Cemetery where tombstones were sometimes mistaken for shining swimming pools by passersby overhead, on their ways to sick-sunny California.

Open up your windows, the trio hollered through the loud speaker.

All of us thrown together in a parking lot—little yellow lines marking slots with numbers same as the cemetery plots beyond.

"That's funny," I said. "Panquake."

Lyra danced, waving both arms, beside her mother. Over there, the girls whose hair is champagne-matted. Mayday just around the bend. There was talk of opening things up, the parks, drive-in movies, maybe. Summer was coming on, maybe the virus doesn't like the heat. It was possible, wasn't it? Somebody said the ultraviolet light kills it dead. Spring was on us. Flowers were blooming, iris bedded in front of our house across the street, just now catching the sun so the yellow stamen stood out against flouncy purple petals. Never seen from this side, they took my breath. There they were, blooming in front of our house, where we'd lived and walked and breathed and birthed a child. Where we'd sheltered in place for fifty straight days in rooms that would no doubt reek of us until kingdom come. This is what they look like from across the street—our purple iris.

Blooming.

What we'd planted that first fall against winter.

Here ends the second part of *White Indians*, the last days of the fourth world and the beginning of the fifth, as prophesized by the Hopi and other tribes. *Omakiya yo, makakija lo. Pilamaya yelo hey.*

Acknowledgements

No one gets from the old world to the new without help. I'd like to thank all who played a part in *White Indians* and *Finisterre*. Miracle workers have appeared all along the way—giving much and asking little. I am grateful. Especially, I'd like to thank Jennifer Barnes at *Raw Dog Screaming Press* for all she's done to see this work through.

And for my fellow pilgrims, some no longer in this world, *buen camino*.

About the Author

Michael Gills is the author of eight books of fiction and nonfiction, including the novel West (Raw Dog Screaming Press, March 2019), Book 3 of the Go Love Quartet. His short story collection *The House Across from The Deaf School* (Texas Review Press, 2016) was nominated for the PEN/Faulkner Prize for Fiction and won the 15 Bytes Utah Book Prize. A 4th collection of short stories, *Burning Down My Father's House*, will be published by Texas Review Press in Fall 2023. Other work has been awarded the Southern Humanities Review's Theodore Hoefner Prize for Fiction, Southern Review's Best Debut of the Year, recognition in the Best American Short Stories and Pushcart Prize Anthology, and inclusion in *New Stories from The South: The Year's Best*. His undergraduate novel writing workshop has been featured in *USA Today*, and several of his students have gone on to publish books of their own. Gills is a Distinguished Honors Professor at the University of Utah, where he lives in the foothills with his wife of thirty-four years, Jill.

www.ingramcontent.com/pod-product-compliance
Lightning Source LLC
Chambersburg PA
CBHW050903180626
46814CB00007B/2865